An Unsolved Murder

Leonard Roger

Contents

1

CHAPTER 1

Barlow Jackson didn't know how to stop Pet's tears. All he could do was continue to hold her until the tears ended.

Breaking up was so very hard to do.

Especially when the breakup involved lifelong childhood sweethearts, two kids who had grown up together as next-door neighbors. As little tykes, they splashed in the same mud puddles. In first grade they walked hand-in-hand to their school bus stop. In middle school Barlow protected her from bullies, and she had given him his first kiss. Then, in high school, she had given him everything else and they became inseparable.

Pet wanted to keep in touch. They could call or text each other every day, but Barlow was pragmatic and understood the reality of the situation. After tonight, they would slowly drift apart, and there existed the very real possibility they would never see each other again. Saying those words out loud was what had led to Pet's tears.

"Don't even think like that. We were meant to end up together," she had said before collapsing into his embrace and sobbing.

Pet would be starting university in the fall. Barlow knew she would accomplish great things in her life. She was intelligent, yet down-to-Earth and beautiful. He was proud of her.

Barlow was just a C student who had a crappy home life. His future was doubtful at best. Their paths were about to diverge, their destinies no longer compatible. If he were selfish, he could ask her to marry him, but he loved her too much to hold her back. Pet needed to be set free.

It wasn't easy though. He hurt too. She was going far away, so he also needed to leave Perry County behind and get away from everything that would remind him of her. Except Barlow knew he could never forget her, his Pet, his best friend and lover.

To counter Pet leaving for university, he had enlisted in the Marines and was Parris Island bound. Who knew what would happen to him if he ever saw combat?

Pet pulled from his embrace and stared into his eyes. He admired, probably for the last time, the light dusting of freckles across her cheeks, the way her nose crinkled when she laughed, her hair the color of corn silk, and her scent.

Her nose started to run from all the crying, and in that instant, Barlow recalled with fondness seeing her often that way as a little girl.

His heart felt as if it would shatter, but he kept a brave face. For her.

Using his shirt tail, he wiped her nose. She emitted a nervous giggle. "You take such good care of me. Who's going to do that now?"

He dropped his gaze. Time to go, because he wouldn't be able to hold it together much longer. "It's late. I have an early flight."

Pet said nothing. She wiped her eyes.

He embraced her one final time. When they separated, he kissed her forehead, turned, and walked off her parent's porch.

Neither of them said goodbye.

Half past midnight and Barlow decided to walk home on the footpath along the Juniata River. He could've taken the road, it being a shorter route. His house and Pet's were the last two located at the end of the rural road, so privacy wasn't an issue. He just needed to be alone to decompress from their farewell.

The full moon guided his way, the August night warm. After finding the forest-lined foot path, he walked slowly, not wanting to trip over the numerous tree roots looming as obstacles. The smell of pines and the gurgling river current usually calmed him, but he was too distraught tonight.

In the distance, Barlow made out the hazy outline of an old weeping willow tree that served as a landmark. The township road made a sharp turn just on the other side of the willow. He got to the tree and stopped, having second thoughts.

Weeping Willow Tree

Had he done the right thing? It wasn't too late. He could still run back to Pet's house, pound on her parent's door, and when she answered tell her he had been temporarily insane. They could make it work. Their love was strong enough.

He took a deep, cleansing breath and squeezed shut his eyes.

No.

Stepping away from the willow, Barlow continued walking. His mind wandered to the one good thing about leaving home. His old man owned a struggling construction business. Things were slow, at least that's what his father always said, using it as an excuse to not pay him.

Over Barlow's continuing objection to the unfairness of the arrangement, the old man would utter, "What you don't get paid in wages is more than made up for through gaining valuable experience in the building trade."

Or some other such bullshit.

Finally, he'd escape from under the old man's thumb and his twentieth century mindset. Barlow actually enjoyed construction, but having been his father's slave left him with a bad taste for that business.

While pondering his fate, Barlow was suddenly overcome with an uneasy feeling. Something seemed out of place. He stood still and looked around. An eerie calm had set in. The only sound, the hiss of water rushing through the river bed.

A pale, ethereal glow illuminated the water ahead of him. The source of the light seemed to come from beneath the ripples. It couldn't be a reflection from the full moon which shone in the water behind him.

The underwater glow drifted his way. Startled by this apparition, he scrambled up the bank and ducked behind a tree. Daring to peek around the trunk, he eyed the ghostly light. After a few moments, he worked out that the strange light hadn't really moved. The rippling current flowing above the glow provided only an illusion of movement.

After calming himself, he approached with caution and...oh, wow! The eerie glow came from two underwater automobile headlights. A sedan lay submerged with only the back half and trunk sticking up from the current.

Barlow guessed someone had driven too fast, didn't make the curve in the road, and ended up in the drink. Could the driver still be in the car? Were there other passengers? He waded in and shouted, "Hello?"

No answer.

Despite the warm August night, his body recoiled from the shock of cold water. He waded onward. The thought of what he might find in the car repelled him, made him want to turn back, run home, and call 911. Let someone else deal with this. But how could he live with himself if someone drowned because he was too cowardly to act?

With a trembling hand, he pulled open the passenger side door. The downstream rush of water caught the opening door and yanked it from Barlow's grasp almost pulling him over. The scene inside the sedan made him wonder if he was dreaming.

A large steamer trunk lay in the back seat. It had sprung open, probably from impact and spilled its contents. Bundles of sopping wet cash had been thrown everywhere. Thousands of dollars' worth, Barlow figured. Maybe a million dollars' worth. The driver was still strapped in his seat with his head underwater.

A Typical Steamer Trunk

Fighting the urge to vomit, Barlow reached beneath the surface and with hands numb from the icy water unlatched the seat belt. He pulled the man across the seat and out the passenger side. He ignored the bills escaping from the car being swept downstream.

His hands had become stiff from the cold, nearly useless, and he could barely maintain his grip on the back of the dead man's collar. Barlow managed to get him to the river's edge. He struggled and pulled the man up the bank and onto level ground.

Moonlight illuminated the corpse's face. A young man, barely older than he was, eyes half closed. Not a local. Barlow didn't recognize him. He rolled the man onto his side to check for a wallet and ID.

Suddenly, the corpse spasmed. A gout of water shot from the man's mouth and he gasped.

2

Chapter 2

The man Barlow thought had drowned was alive!

Startled, Barlow jumped backward, tripped, and fell onto his butt. He crawled to the man who lay on his side suffering from fits of coughing.

He got to his knees and bent over the man, trying to figure out how he could help. "You're going to be okay."

The man stared at him, his face porcelain white with bulging Gollum-sized eyes.

"My house is nearby. I'm going for help. I'll be right back." Barlow ran to the house as fast as the uneven terrain would allow.

He burst through the backdoor, breathless and shivering. At the foot of the staircase, he yelled up toward his parents' bedroom, "Mom, Dad, there's been an accident. A car is in the river. A man has been hurt."

His mother appeared in a nightgown at the top of the staircase. "What did you say?"

Barlow repeated the news and ran to the phone, dialed 911.

He heard his mother shout, "Forrest, you'd better wake up."

By the time Barlow reported the accident, his father had come downstairs, fully dressed. "Where is the wreck?"

"Just this side of the weeping willow tree. The car is in the stream, and I pulled the driver up onto the bank. By now he's probably in shock."

"Better take a blanket for the poor man," his mother said. She grabbed a quilt from the hallway closet and handed it to her husband.

His father started for the door.

"I'm coming with you," Barlow said.

"No, boy, you're soaked and liable to get sick if you go back outside. You have an early flight tomorrow. Go to bed. I'll take care of this."

Did the old man actually think he would be able to sleep after everything that happened to him tonight?

His mother laid a hand on his shoulder. "Change out of those wet things, Barlow. I'll heat up some milk for you. It'll help you sleep."

He climbed the stairs to his room and stripped, took a quick hot shower, and pulled on some sweats. He returned to the kitchen and sat, waiting for his father to return.

"Drink your milk. Your father might be gone a long time. Then you should go to bed." Barlow noted her diplomatic tone. His mother had mastered the art of diplomacy; it was the only way she could deal with her husband. Although his father never raised a hand to her, Barlow had often witnessed his verbal tirades.

The last time his father used a belt on him, Barlow had been twelve. Although he no longer suffered from beatings, the old man abused him in other ways. He wouldn't allow Barlow to get a driver's license, made him haul bundles of shingles up a ladder all day long at construction sites, and had kept him from engaging in after school activities with his friends.

If it weren't for Pet, Barlow figured he never would've survived until graduation.

"I'm not going to bed. The cops will probably want to talk with me since I was first on the scene."

His mother considered his words and nodded. "I suppose that makes sense."

Barlow dozed at the kitchen table while waiting. His mother woke him when his father returned. The man looked between the two of them and shook his head. "The police measured the skid marks. The dumb ass was going too fast to make the turn. Ended up in the river."

Just as Barlow had suspected. "Is he going to be all right?"

His father shot him a sideways glance. "The man's dead. Drowned."

Barlow took a moment to process what his father had said. "What do you mean? I pulled him from the car and up onto the bank. He was recovering when I left him."

"Don't you go making up lies. That man was buckled into his seat and underwater. I watched as the EMTs pulled him out."

"That can't be. What about all the money?"

"What money?"

Barlow scoffed. "A steamer trunk filled with bills."

His father's face reddened. "I don't know what game you're playing, but by god, you'd better drop your disrespectful tone."

Barlow pushed back from the table, stood, and glared at his old man. "I don't play games. I saw what I saw."

"I don't know what you think you saw, but I'm telling you the man driving that car is dead and there is no steamer trunk. No money."

Barlow thought about it. Was it possible? Could his old man really be that much of a bastard? "Who got to the scene first, you or the cops?"

"I did."

"How much time did you have before the police arrived?"

His father narrowed his eyes and took a step forward. "What are you trying to say, boy?"

His mother stepped between them. "Forrest, you've been out in the night air a long time. Let me pour you a cup of coffee."

Barlow ignored his mother's attempt to de-escalate the situation and continued the staring contest with his father. "You go on and on about how slow things are with the business. An infusion of cash would solve a lot of problems, wouldn't it?"

His father's jaw trembled and his face turned beet red. Barlow wondered from anger or guilt? The man's words came out as a growl. "You'd better watch what you say. You may be eighteen, but I can still put you on your ass."

"Think so? Why don't you go ahead and try?"

In a panicky voice, his mother said, "That's enough. Both of you stop this."

Except Barlow didn't want to stop. This showdown had been brewing for a long time. "Why are your clothes soaked, Dad? Did that happen when you waded into the river to steal the trunk?"

The old man glared but said nothing.

"Let me guess," Barlow went on. "The guy on the bank objected to your taking his cash. Things got physical—"

"—Not as physical as things are about to get—"

"—But in his weakened state, you easily overpowered him. Then what? You held him under the water? Put him back in the driver's seat? No one would ever know, right? Where did you hide the money?"

The old man took a stuttering breath but said nothing.

Barlow went on. "You killed him, didn't you? You staged the body and hid the money."

His mother looked at him in horror. "You can't believe your father would do such a thing."

"Can't I? Why has he suddenly gone quiet? Why won't he defend himself? Probably because he can't."

Barlow's father pointed at the door. "Gather your things and get out. I don't ever want to see you again. You're no longer welcome in this house."

3

Chapter 3

Ten Years Later

Barlow sucked in a deep breath of fresh, crisp air, held it in his lungs for a few seconds, and slowly exhaled.

"What the hell are you doing, Jackson," his boss, Irv Washington asked, "practicing Yoga or something?" Irv placed his hands on his hips. The big man with his dark chocolate skin and shaved head made an imposing figure, but Barlow knew he had a heart of gold.

In the background, a pair of carpenters hammered wall studs into place, the rat-a-tat of their two hammers pounded nails in near perfect syncopation. "I'm just enjoying the smell of fresh cut lumber."

"You're aware we're behind schedule, right? It's November and we need to get eight more of these new townhouses under roof before the snow flies."

Barlow nodded. "I hear you, boss, but I can't lay shingles until Calvin and Tommy finish the plywood sheeting over the roof trusses."

"What? You mean they're behind again too?" Irv took a step back and peered to the rooftop, holding a hand over his brow to shield his eyes from the sun. "Hey, you deadbeats, get a move on. You're costing me money."

The two men glanced down, waved, and began working faster.

Irv cursed and said, "Damn rookies."

"Don't sweat it, boss, I'll climb up there and give them a hand."

"You shouldn't have to. It's their job, not yours."

As Barlow grabbed the rungs of the ladder to begin his climb, Irv asked, "You didn't forget about our meeting tonight, right?"

Barlow always acted put out but secretly enjoyed the periodic dinner meetings with his boss to discuss progress on their various construction projects. "If you insist."

"I insist."

"Then you're buying."

Barlow agreed to meet Irv Washington at The Eight Ball, a downtown Columbus, Ohio sports bar located less than a mile from his apartment. The place served great tavern food, and during the rare occasion when he had one too many, he had the option of walking home.

After entering the establishment, Barlow's eyes adjusted to the dark, smoky atmosphere and found his boss sitting at a table viewing a large screen television. The man was a die hard college football fan.

Irv paid rapt attention to the broadcast and flinched when Barlow approached and laid a hand on his shoulder. "Hey, boss. What are you watching?"

"Rebroadcast of the past weekend Buckeyes game against Penn State."

Barlow hadn't seen the game but recalled the outcome. "They trounced the Nittany Lions and at Beaver Stadium too."

Irv's broad smile lit up his face. "Yeah, man. It was glorious."

Caroline, the Eight Ball's night manager approached, all smiles, and set Barlow's usual in front of him, a local craft beer. "How was your day?"

"Good. Better than most. How's your's going?"

The slight-built, energetic young woman rolled her dark eyes. "Don't know yet. My day's just getting started."

He used his foot to push out a chair.

Caroline shook her head. "Can't join you. Connie called in sick again, so I have to take her place as waitress. Pool tournament later tonight means we're going to be mobbed."

The news dampened Barlow's mood. "You should fire Connie."

She shrugged and walked away.

Irv cleared his throat which got Barlow's attention. The man stared at him with a raised eyebrow. "So, you and Caroline, eh?"

The two of them dated. He liked Caroline a lot and pondered if they might have a future together. Barlow was reluctant to commit, because he inevitably ended up comparing potential partners to his best friend and lover from his teen years. He knew it wasn't fair of him. No woman would ever be able to measure up to Pet.

"Since you ain't talking, I'll get right to the point," Irv said. "I want to make you my partner in the business. You're my most senior laborer with the most experience. You work rings around the rest of the crew and know as much about the construction trade as I do. I'm getting older and the work is getting harder for me to manage by myself."

Barlow felt flattered. He was getting older too, maybe time to settle down and start a family. Maybe with Caroline. "Thank you, Irv. Let me give it some serious thought."

"Yeah, do that."

He didn't know what would've happened if Irv hadn't hired him when he arrived in Columbus after his tour-of-duty with the Marines. Barlow had no desire to return to Perry County, Pennsylvania. He didn't want to ever see his father again, and his absence protected Pet and her family from what his father might do if he suspected the neighbors knew what Barlow knew. He didn't know where else to go, so he had tacked a map of the U.S. on the barracks wall and thrown a dart. It had stuck in Ohio.

Caroline returned. "What'll you be having to eat?"

Irv didn't hesitate. "Cheese steak grinder with onion rings."

Barlow didn't feel all that hungry. "Give me a Reuben, please. Side order of coleslaw."

She didn't bother writing it down. Caroline was one of those waitresses who remembered everything her customers ordered. She amazed Barlow with her ability to keep it all straight, especially on busy nights like this one. She was an intelligent, hard-working young lady who by some miracle really liked him. He would be a fool not to pursue her.

After she walked away, Irv said, "Another reason I wanted to meet with you is to get an opinion. When we finish our current project, we have no work until next spring."

That was typical, Barlow knew. Most years he and the crew got laid off during winter.

Irv took a drink of beer and set down his mug. "I received a call from Quad Lakes Construction. They won the contract to renovate those old factories in the Brewery District into apartments. They called to find out if we had an interest in being a subcontractor."

Steady work during the winter would be great, but, "Quad Lakes Construction has a sketchy reputation, rumors of collusion with city hall to secure large-scale urban renewal jobs like the one you're talking about. Will they pay us on time, and do you want to associate with a business like that?"

Irv smiled. "Your insight is another reason why I want you as a partner."

Barlow's phone vibrated. He plucked it from his hip pocket and recognized the number. His mother. "Hello?"

"Barlow, uh, I have bad news."

He gripped the phone tight to his ear. "What is it? Are you sick? Is something wrong with you?"

"No. Not me. I'm fine. It's your father. He passed away yesterday evening."

Barlow felt nothing, and it didn't bother him one bit. "What did he die of? Meanness?"

His mother gasped. "Barlow, the man was your father."

"Sorry, mother."

"Listen to me, son. Your father left a will. His lawyer called me asking for your contact information."

After his mother divorced his father, she had remarried and moved to Texas. The lawyer must have had a tough time tracking them down.

She continued, "Your self-imposed exile has gone on long enough. With your father's passing, there's no longer a reason for you to stay away from Perry County."

He heard her take a deep breath. "Barlow, there's a situation involving your father's estate. You need to go home."

4

Chapter 4

Above photo: New Bloomfield, PA square with courthouse and monument.

Pennsylvania State Police Trooper Petronia Henning cruised along PA route 34 through the Borough of Newport, PA toward the county seat of New Bloomfield. Residents there had been complaining about excessive speeding. Last week a drunken out-of-towner lost control of his sedan, left the roadway, and had nearly run into the courthouse building.

Since criminal court was in session this morning, the normally sleepy little town would experience a marked increase in traffic and pedestrian activity. Petronia had been assigned to patrol the area and enforce the speed limit.

She hated speed enforcement. Although she recognized it as a part of her job, long hours operating a radar gun bored her. Not that she had any desire to plunge into a firefight with violent criminals, but she sometimes wished things were a little livelier. Fat chance of that happening in relatively peaceful, rural Perry County.

"Careful what you wish for," she mumbled while checking the vehicle inspection sticker of an oncoming SUV passing by in the other lane. In reality, she was grateful for being posted here in the county where she had grown up.

Petronia slowed when entering the borough and navigated her cruiser around the monument in the center of town. She parallel parked a block from the courthouse and checked the time, five after eight in the morning.

She grabbed her trooper hat and set it on her head, noticing how tight it fit. Her regulation pixie cut needed a trim.

Credit: Photo of a female PA State Police Trooper from website: www.patrooper.com

A dump truck roared past so fast that the wind in its wake rocked her cruiser. She saw the driver jam on the breaks before careening around the monument.

"That idiot is going to kill someone." She fired up the cruiser, switched on the lights and siren, and gave chase.

The dump truck traveled nearly a half-mile before she caught up. The driver pulled over onto a wide shoulder after passing the cutoff to the Perry County prison.

Petronia called in her location to dispatch, jammed the hat more securely on her head, fixed the chin strap, and climbed out of the cruiser. While shielded by the door, she unbuttoned the flap to her handgun as a precaution and took her time approaching the driver door while assessing the situation.

An oversize side mirror allowed her to see the reflection of the man behind the wheel. He yanked sunglasses from his face and scowled.

Too late, she realized she should have slipped into her jacket. She walked face first into a cold November gust. Dead leaves streamed by her. The wind stung her eyes making them water.

The dump truck sat high off the road making it difficult for her to inspect the inside of the cab. She'd have to be extra vigilant.

The driver powered down his window. White, male, he looked to be in his thirties, wavy red hair, wearing a wool shirt. When the man saw her, his scowl turned into a smirk. "Didn't know you was a woman."

She ignored his quip. "Sir, I'm going to need to see your driver's license, vehicle registration, and proof of insurance, please."

He shook his head. "A female statey, and a pretty one at that."

She needed to gain this man's respect. Best way to do that would be to ignore his sexist comments—no matter how much it pissed her off to do so—and maintain her professional demeanor. She cleared her throat and tried speaking as authoritatively as possible over the roaring wind. "License, registration, and proof of insurance."

The driver wore a surprised expression and pointed a finger at his chest. "Why? Was I over?"

"Sir, I'm not going to ask you again."

He held up both hands in the classic don't shoot me pose. "Okay, babe, no problem."

She entertained the fantasy of pulling her gun and shooting the asshole in the face. "My name is Trooper Henning, or if you prefer, you can call me ma'am.

He scoffed and pulled down his sun visor. From a plastic document holder attached to the back of the visor he removed some papers, studied them, and reached them out the window. In the split second before she closed her hand around the documents, he let them slip through his fingers. The wind carried them away with the leaves.

He chuckled. "Oops."

She watched the papers blow across the street and into the weeds.

The man leered at her. "Now look what you did. Guess you better go get 'em before they get lost."

Petronia could imagine his delight at seeing her running around like a little girl, chasing down his credentials. Wasn't going to happen. "Sir, I'm going to need you to step out of your vehicle."

He sniffed the air. "It's cold out there."

She shivered, not knowing whether it was from the chill air or from adrenaline coursing through her body. She rested a hand on the butt of her handgun. "Out of the truck. Now."

He twisted in his seat and leaned both of his forearms on the open window frame. He looked down at her. "I got a better idea. 'Stead of me stepping out, why don't you climb into my nice warm cab with me? We can get better acquainted."

Having run out of patience, she grabbed the dump truck door handle and yanked it open. The driver, having leaned his weight against the window frame, lost his balance and started to fall out. Petronia helped gravity. She grabbed his wool shirt and wrenched the man from his seat. He tumbled face first into the cinders of the road shoulder.

The man shouted obscenities, but before he could get up, she pinned him by placing both knees on his back. She grabbed an arm and cuffed his wrist.

He screamed and yelled, "Not so rough. I have a torn rotator cuff. Get off me."

She ignored him and grabbed his other wrist, cuffed it. Next, she kicked his legs apart and patted him down for weapons.

The man cursed, calling her nasty names. "Am I under arrest, or what?"

"Yeah, you're under arrest." After a pause, she added, "Sir."

5

Chapter 5

Central Pennsylvania weather was typical for November, raw and rainy. Barlow pulled into the parking lot of The Inn of The Dancing Bear located near Loysville. He remembered the place from his childhood. His father drove him by it many times during trips to and from a sawmill in the town of Blain, but they never stopped. His father didn't approve of places that served alcohol. The old man was in no way religious, he just didn't approve of drinking or smoking or anything that fit his definition of squandering time. To him, every waking moment had to be productive.

He recalled one particular incident that always stuck with him. The Hennings invited Barlow to Pet's tenth birthday party. He knew better than to ask permission. His mother would've let him go, but she had no say in the matter. No wonder she eventually divorced his father after Barlow had joined the Marines.

Barlow lied to his parents, telling them he needed extra schooling and would stay after hours for science tutoring. Instead, he rode the bus as usual and got off, walking with Pet to attend her afternoon party.

It would've worked except his father happened to drive by and see them. The old man pulled over and asked Barlow for an explanation. Barlow had no choice but to tell him the truth.

His father pulled the belt from his pant loops. "Extra schooling? I'll give you extra schooling right across your backside for lying."

And he did. Right in front of Pet. He still remembered the look of horror on his little friend's face.

Barlow gripped the steering wheel. "The bastard should have died a long time ago." He sat in the parking spot, wipers on low. The inn was located a half-hour drive from his childhood home. Close enough. He waited until the rain eased to a steady drizzle. He shut off the motor to his van and climbed out.

The gravel lot crunched beneath his work boots as he walked toward the entrance. Why did he feel so nervous? Barlow chalked it up to being close to home. The old man may be dead, but his aura still infected the atmosphere. He grabbed the door handle and pulled. The heavy old door swung open easily on smooth hinges. The workmanship impressed him.

He paused after entering to allow his eyes to adjust. No one manned the greeting station and a sign read:

Bad Moon Rising played on the jukebox. The song fit his mood.

He checked the time, a few minutes past two. Too late for lunch and too early for the dinner crowd. Probably explained why the place wasn't busy.

A long bar ran against the far wall. He headed that way and took a seat. Two guys wearing Carhartt overalls sat a few stools away discussing the weather. An old-timer wearing a dirty hunting coat sat at the end of the bar, beer mug in hand.

The old-timer looked at him with suspicion. He had a weird facial tick that made it look as if he couldn't stop winking.

The bartender appeared from the kitchen carrying a rack of glasses. He glanced at the old-timer. "You ready for another one, Twitchy?"

Twitchy re-focused onto the bartender and nodded.

When the bartender saw Barlow, he set the rack of glasses on the bar and approached. "What's your pleasure?"

Barlow eyed the labels on the tap handles. "I'll try a Yuengling Lager."

"Glass or mug?"

"Mug."

From a cooler, the bartender removed a frosted mug and filled it from the tap. He grabbed a coaster from a stack and set it in front of Barlow along with the mug. "Don't believe I've seen you around before."

"My first time here."

The bartender extended a hand. "I'm Trevor Dunne. I run this inn along with my wife, Jill."

Reaching across the bar, Barlow shook Trevor's hand and introduced himself. The bartender had a firm grip and a scrutinizing gaze that he had trouble holding.

Trevor leaned against the bar. "Where are you from?"

"Originally from the Millerstown area. I live in Ohio now."

"What brings you back to Perry County?"

Caroline often complained how being friendly was a necessary part of the wait staff's job. Taking that into account, Barlow couldn't fault Trevor for wanting to make conversation, but he didn't feel like sharing his life story. He decided to be stingy with his response hoping the man would lose interest. "My father recently passed away. I'm here to settle his estate."

Trevor took a half-step back. "Sorry to hear that."

Barlow wasn't sorry but rather annoyed it fell to him to deal with the remnants of the old man's life, a final dig by his father from beyond the grave. "Thanks, but we weren't close." Not by a long shot.

Twitchy held up his empty mug. "Hey, where's my refill?"

"Hang on, I'm coming." Trevor walked away.

Barlow swiveled on his bar stool to take in the establishment. An unusual walk-in sized stone fireplace adorned the wall to the left of the bar. No fire burned there now, but a stack of logs lay nearby ready to go.

The fireplace gave the place a rustic vibe. The building's walls constructed of thick logs added to the comfy atmosphere. Thick trees were rare nowadays; he guessed the structure was at least a hundred years old. A dining area with twenty or so tables sat to the right of the bar. Between the bar and the dining room, a bandstand was located adjacent to a parquet dance floor.

Barlow swiveled back to the bar and studied the rivulets of condensation trailing down the side of his beer mug. It reminded him of the fast running river during the night he had discovered the submerged man.

Being here and dredging up past memories had Barlow feeling uneasy. He downed his beer.

Trevor walked his way. "Another?"

"Yeah, one more."

The bartender refilled his mug and used a rag to wipe the bar. He plopped down a fresh coaster before replacing the refilled mug.

Barlow wrapped his hand around the mug handle. "You have any rooms available?"

Trevor cocked his head. "You're not staying at your late father's house?"

He didn't like the bartender getting into his business but realized it was a reasonable question. "No."

Trevor didn't press him on the matter. "How many nights do you expect to stay?"

"Not sure. Depends how long it'll take to settle things."

"Deer season starts the Monday after Thanksgiving. You can have a room until then, but we're booked solid with hunters after that."

Thanksgiving was six days from today. Barlow intended to be long gone before then. "No problem."

"It will take housekeeping an hour or so to get your room ready. Would you like to see a menu and have a late lunch while you wait?"

"Can't. I have a meeting. Be back later."

"Just to let you know, being a Friday, we have live music this evening."

"What kind of music?"

"Nothing too wild. Usually two or three musicians playing country or bluegrass. I mention it so you're not surprised by the big crowd when you return. Also, I need you to know that unless you are an exceptionally sound sleeper, you won't get much shuteye until the band quits at midnight."

Barlow drank the rest of his beer, paid his tab, and finalized arrangements for the room. He stepped into a fine mist as he exited the inn. The rain had eased, but overcast skies threatened heavier rain again later.

While driving, he made a mental list of things to accomplish during the next few days: visit with the attorney, go through the old man's accounts to settle up any unpaid debts, and pay a visit to his father's employees.

That should do it. Afterwards, he would make a quick exit from the county never to return. This place wasn't his home anymore.

6

CHAPTER 6

It drizzled rain the whole way from the Dancing Bear to the office of his father's lawyer, Lincoln Chronister.

The first thing to strike Barlow upon entering the attorney's office was the smell of old law books. Bookcases full of the volumes lined the entire rear wall.

The man extended a hand. "Call me Link."

Barlow shook his hand and automatically responded with, "Pleased to meet you."

Link pointed to one of the leather chairs surrounding a small conference table. "Have a seat."

Barlow did as the man asked. Link sat opposite him and cleared his throat. "Let's get started." The lawyer opened a file folder and pulled out a document. "I can read your father's will for you verbatim, but it contains a lot of legalese. Is it okay if I cut to the chase and summarize the salient points?"

"Fine by me."

"Good. Your father stipulated his wish to be cremated with no viewing of the body and no funeral service. You can have his ashes if that's what you want."

Barlow scoffed. "Yeah, right."

Link tapped the document with his index finger. "To be clear, are you telling me you don't want your father's remains?"

"Correct. I don't want his remains."

"His funeral expenses have been prepaid, so I don't expect any deductions from the estate will be necessary for those services." Link leaned back in his chair. "Your father wrote your mother out of his will. He made mention how the divorce settlement more than covered anything he would ever owe her."

"That's a stretch. My mother gave that man the best years of her life."

The lawyer stared at Barlow. "Young man, your father has left his entire estate to you, the house, the business, all of his possessions." He slid a ring of keys across the tabletop toward him. "These keys are for your father's house, his construction office, and all of his vehicles and equipment."

Barlow wasn't sure he heard properly. "What?"

"You are the sole beneficiary of the estate."

Barlow's heart raced, not with excitement over the inheritance, but with horror. He slid his chair back and stood. "I want none of it."

Link's mouth hung open. "In all my years, I never...you need to think this through."

"My father has men who have worked with him. Good men who have been loyal. Why isn't he passing the construction business on to them?"

The lawyer shrugged.

"That bastard," Barlow uttered. "Why did he do this to me?"

"Maybe it's his way of making amends," Link said. "Don't do anything rash, Barlow. A lot of money is involved."

"I don't want it."

The attorney closed the folder and slid it to the side. "I've been your father's attorney since before you were born. I don't presume to know what happened between the two of you, but I knew Forrest well enough to tell you he had a keen business sense. If he left his possessions to you, it's because he knew you would do right by them."

Barlow scoffed. "I haven't seen the old man for ten years. How does he know what I'm capable of doing?"

"He must have figured you would make a good steward for his construction business."

Unable to wrap his mind around his father's intent, Barlow uttered, "I never wanted this."

Link sighed. "You're just like him, stubborn as hell. Look, Barlow, maybe in death this is your father's way of reaching out to you. In any case, like it or not, it's all yours now."

Barlow still couldn't believe it. "Does that mean I can do whatever I want with his stuff?"

"It will take a few months to clear probate, but bottom line is you have sole discretion. You are free to dispose of your father's property as you see fit, of course, as long as you keep it legal. Don't burn down the house." The attorney let slip a nervous chuckle after saying that. He rose from his seat, a signal Barlow took to mean the meeting was over.

The landscape hadn't changed much during Barlow's ten-year absence. A few new houses had popped up along the ridges, and more land had been posted off-limits to hunters.

The rain grew ever more intense making a deafening racket as it drummed against the roof of the cavernous van. Barlow switched the wipers on high. In the decreasing visibility, he almost missed the school bus shelter that served as a landmark for the turnoff onto the township road.

Mr. Henning, Pet's father had built the small shelter there for his daughter which she shared with Barlow. He recalled scrunching close with her under its roof on freezing, winter mornings while waiting for the school bus, and the things they did there after they got older.

He felt a dull ache in his gut at the thought of her. Wherever Pet might be in this world, he hoped she was happy.

The little shelter had fallen into a state of disrepair. While driving by, Barlow noticed some of the shingles had torn away, a few of the wall boards appeared rotted, and the entire structure needed a fresh coat of paint.

Ten years ago, their two houses stood alone at the far end of the county road. Several new homes lined the township road now. If kids lived here, he wondered why nobody bothered to fix the little shelter.

Barlow slowed as he approached Pet's childhood home. It looked the same as he remembered with its big front porch and swing. The mailbox still bore the name: Henning. Her parents must still live there. Maybe she did too. Probably not. Pet had been destined to get away from Perry County and probably lived in a big city somewhere.

A few seconds later, Barlow came to the dangerous curve in the road. The trees grew thick here, a mixture of poplar and oaks interspersed with scrubby redbuds and dogwoods. He searched for the lone weeping willow, the spot near where the vehicle had entered the river in what seemed like a lifetime ago.

He drifted the van forward. The willow eventually came into view. "There you are."

Barlow gunned the motor, left the willow tree behind, and approached the house of his youth, a two-story colonial. He pulled into the driveway and studied the old place but didn't get out. In that moment, he made a snap decision. He'd turn the keys over to an auctioneer. Let someone else deal with the problem. Whatever money he could get for the place he would give to his mother.

Suddenly tired, Barlow backed out of the driveway. He looked forward to his bed at the inn and a long night's sleep.

7

CHAPTER 7

Petronia sat on the sofa wrapped in a bathrobe. She had just taken a hot shower and downed two aspirin with a glass of wine hoping to dull the ache in her head. The television broadcast the news at six, but she wasn't paying attention, only having the set turned on to keep her company.

Leaning back on the sofa, she closed her eyes and squeezed the bridge of her nose. The aspirin was kicking in. Her headache had faded to a dull throb.

Her bad day started during the arrest of Slay Gunther, the chucklehead dump truck driver. Imagine naming a kid Slay! When he first told her that, she felt sure he was continuing to mess with her, but sure enough, that had been the name on his license. After settling him into the back of her patrol car, he had laughed at her as she searched the weeds for his credentials, hooting every time she had bent over.

To top it off, the sky had chosen that moment to open and pour rain, adding to Slay's delight while he watched her. While driving the man to the state police station in Newport, he had screamed the entire time, calling her every vile name he could think of until his imagination ran dry. Then he shouted threats, promising to call the ACLU. Although a screened partition separated them, the spittle from his screaming peppered the skin on the back of her neck.

Petronia strived to maintain a professional attitude as a law enforcement officer, but she couldn't help feeling a deep sense of satisfaction, even pleasure, when marching Slay Gunther through the station to a holding cell.

She detailed the incident to her barracks commander, Lieutenant Martin Jardine, and explained how she was going to throw the book at him. He told her she had performed her duty well, but...

From experience, Petronia knew nothing good ever came after her lieutenant uttered the word, "but."

He didn't want her to go overboard by stacking too many charges. It would give the appearance of being overzealous, if not outright vindictive. The district justice would see through it and toss most of the charges anyway.

Although Petronia understood his logic, it still frustrated her. She needed to blow off some steam and an idea came to her. It had been a long time since she went out and had some fun. Twisting the wedding band on her finger, Petronia realized she hadn't partied since her divorce from Charlie.

Her cousin, Maggie, had been begging her for weeks to visit. If she was free tomorrow evening, maybe the two of them could enjoy a girls' night out. She grabbed her cell phone and pulled up her cousin's number.

After the sixth ring, Petronia was about to hang up when she heard a grouchy, "Hello."

"Maggie? It's Pet."

"Oh, darn, I had just gotten to sleep."

Petronia checked the clock. "At half past six?"

"Sorry, cuz, I'm fighting a bitch of a cold. Sore throat too."

Petronia could hear in her voice how stuffed up she was. "Gosh, I'm sorry. I didn't know. Look, forget it. We can talk some other time."

"Wait. I'm wide awake now. What's going on?"

Petronia told her cousin about the arrest of Slay Gunther.

Maggie chuckled and then started coughing. After catching her breath, she said, "Slay? You're kidding."

"Nope, that's the guy's name."

Maggie started coughing again.

"I'm gonna go," Petronia said. "You need your rest."

"Not until you tell me the real reason you called."

Maggie was like that. She had a sixth sense and could tell when something bothered her. "I was wondering if you wanted to go out with me tomorrow night, but of course, that's out of the question now since you're sick." While talking, she twisted the wedding band on her finger, a nervous habit she found difficult to break.

"I can't go, but you should," Maggie said. "Go by yourself."

"Not without you. It wouldn't be fun."

"It would be fun if some great looking guy asked you to dance and then...you know...took you home."

Petronia scoffed. "I should be so lucky."

"C'mon, Pet, you're totally hot. I'll bet you get picked up within the first five minutes."

Was she totally hot? If so, why had Charlie left her for another woman? What stung even worse, the other woman wasn't younger but four years older than she was. "I'd feel weird going by myself."

"You are a law enforcement officer. You have nothing to be afraid of."

"I didn't say I was afraid. I said I'd feel weird." Really weird if some guy she had previously arrested tried to hit on her.

"Pet, it's been almost two years since your divorce. You need to put yourself out there."

Easy for Maggie to say. She was happily married to a great guy who doted on her. Charlie had often confessed his love, but he had never doted on her. "I'll think about it."

Maggie coughed. "Don't think about it. Do it. Then call me, and tell me all about how things went."

"Like I said, I'll think about it."

"Oh, and Pet...I know you continue to wear that wedding band as a shield to keep men away."

After the divorce, she had sworn off men until enough time passed for her to get over the pain. It had been the second time in her life she had suffered because of a man who had loved her and left her. Petronia thought back to a long-ago summer. To the first time. She wiped away a tear that had suddenly leaked from her eye. The ring made most men think twice about approaching her, but as Maggie reminded her, it had been almost two years now.

She still wasn't sure enough time had passed to risk making herself vulnerable again.

Maggie coughed. "Are you still there?"

"Yes."

"When you go out tomorrow night. Be sure to leave your ring at home. It's time you tossed it into the back of a dresser drawer where it will be forgotten."

8

CHAPTER 8

Barlow pushed open the door to his room at the inn. He noted with surprise how clean it was, furnished with an antique dresser and a double bed set atop a large braided rug. Quaint. The room matched the rustic vibe of the inn's bar and dining area. Above the headboard hung a painting of white-tail deer grazing against the backdrop of high snowy peaks. Wasn't typical of a hotel painting he would find in downtown Columbus. Having to share a common bathroom with other guests made him feel awkward, but he figured he could adapt.

After plopping his overnight bag on the dresser, Barlow kicked off his work boots and tested the mattress. He lay back on the pillow and closed his eyes. No TV in the room, but it made no difference. He was tired. If he went to sleep now, he could get an early start in the morning.

Barlow had set the alarm app on his phone for six. The Friday night band Trevor had warned him about kept him awake until well after midnight. After that, he slept fitfully until giving up at five. He sat on the side of the bed. A dead silence hung in the air. None of the other lodgers stirred.

He yawned. What were the chances he'd be able to get a cup of coffee at this hour? None, he knew. The restaurant downstairs wouldn't open for a couple hours and there was no coffee pot in the room. Unlike Columbus where there was a Starbucks on every corner, the nearest coffee would be more than twenty miles away at one of the all-night truck stops located near the town of Carlisle.

An advantage to getting up early, there would be no competition to use one of the bathrooms at each end of the hall.

Pulling on his trousers, Barlow grabbed his toiletries, room key, and shuffled to the nearest shower.

At six, he figured Lester Cunningham, his father's foreman at the Jackson Construction Company would be awake. He punched the man's number into his phone. Les answered right away sounding chipper. Barlow introduced himself and decided to get straight to the point. "I'm wondering if we could meet sometime this morning?"

Les took a moment before responding. "I remember you. You were a good worker as a kid. I'm sorry about your father. All of us at the company are."

"It's Saturday, but if you could grant me a few minutes of your time, I'd appreciate it."

After an awkward silence, Les asked, "What's going to happen, Barlow? None of us know what your father planned in the event of his passing. Besides myself, there are five other men on the payroll, and we're all nervous. Some of the guys are putting out feelers with other companies."

"That's why I want to meet with you. I'll explain everything."

"In that case, come on over to the house. I'll be waiting."

"Look, Les, I prefer to meet you at the office, because I'm going to need to look at the company financials."

"I'll be there in half an hour."

Barlow ended the call and headed toward the small office located just outside Millerstown. He recalled how his father spent little time there. It's where he did his paperwork and met with clients. The plain building was nothing more than a dressed-up modular unit, but it served its purpose.

Pulling his van into the parking lot, he spied a pickup truck and assumed it belonged to Les. The office door was unlocked, so Barlow walked in. Les greeted him and handed him coffee in a Styrofoam cup.

Barlow sipped. "Thanks, man, I needed this."

Les looked exactly as Barlow had remembered him, short and a bit stocky, except now he had graying hair at his temples. They sat across from each other on metal folding chairs at a rickety old wooden table. After a few minutes of chitchat, Barlow told Les about the will and how he now owned his father's business.

Les sat back in his chair and regarded him. "I gotta say I'm surprised given that you and your father had such a falling out."

"You're not half as surprised as I am."

"I thought maybe he'd turn the business over to your mother, despite the fact that they divorced. As far as I know your father had nobody else in his life."

"He had you and his employees."

Les blew across the top of his hot coffee cup before speaking. "The thought did cross my mind that he might take care of us somehow, maybe arrange for a buyout."

"Did my father ever tell you why he and I had a falling out?"

"Nope. All he said was we wouldn't be seeing you around anymore. I knew better than to ask him why." Les leaned forward in his chair. "Would you care to tell me about it?"

"Maybe, but not now."

Les cocked his head. "What's going to happen with the business?"

"You were with my father since the beginning. Only God knows how you were able to put up with that man all these years. I'll figure out some way to take care of you and the crew. It's the least I can do."

Worry lines creased Les's forehead. "There's a lot of expensive construction equipment tied up with the business, building materials, and even this office. I have a kid in college and my daughter's wedding to pay for. I wouldn't have the kind of cash it would take to buy you out, if that's what you had in mind."

Barlow thought about it. "The attorney told me it would take a few months for everything to go through probate. Let's not worry until that happens. I'm sure we'll be able to come up with some sort of arrangement."

"That sounds great, but there's another problem."

"What's that?"

Les rubbed the whiskers on his face. "Like I told you over the phone. The guys are nervous and some of them are likely to jump ship. That'll ruin our business due to ongoing contract obligations."

Barlow sat back in his chair. His boss in Ohio, Irv Washington, was looking for work for his construction crew, and he wanted Barlow to be his partner. Could this be a mutually beneficial opportunity? "If your guys continue to work, are there enough funds to make payroll?"

"I think so but can't say for sure. Your father kept the company financials strictly to himself. He never shared any of that with me."

Of course, the old man wouldn't trust anybody.

Les continued, "I can tell you, though, that in all the years I worked for him, he never missed a payroll."

"I need to examine the books, financial statements, payroll records, everything."

"Your father kept everything in the files." Les bobbed his head toward the direction of a bank of locked file cabinets. "He's the only one who had the keys. It's all on paper. Your dad was old school, did everything by hand and didn't put anything into a computer."

Easier to hide things that way, Barlow figured. "I have the keys." He removed the ring of keys the attorney had given him and tried them until he found the one fitting the file cabinets. He would finally get to the bottom of things. The records would show where any sudden cash infusions came from. He would spot any irregularities and figure out how his father laundered all the cash he had stolen from the poor bastard who died in the river.

He turned back to Les. "I want to pick your brain about how things were around here ten years ago."

"Ten years ago?" Les closed his eyes as if searching his memory.

Barlow returned to the table, took his seat, and gave the man time to think.

When Les opened his eyes, he said, "Actually, I recall ten years ago very well. That's when the business really took off, and, uh, I believe that's right around the time you left. Your father landed a housing development job outside of New Bloomfield. It's the largest residential development in Perry County and a financial windfall for the company."

Barlow remained silent a moment while processing that information. "My mother corresponded with me while I was in the Marines. She told me about the project, but she never made it sound like such a big deal."

"It wasn't just a big deal, it was a huge deal. Three hundred homes during the past ten years, and the developer has granted us a contract extension to build ten more each year for the next three years. That's the obligation I was referring to earlier."

Doing the math in his head, Barlow realized how that would have brought a shit-ton of cash into the business. He suddenly felt uneasy. Could he have been wrong about his father? "I should find all the details in the financial records." He went to the office Keurig machine and popped in another K-cup for a second cup of coffee. "No reason for you to hang around, Les. Tell the guys I'll make sure they get paid. Other than a change in ownership, everything will continue as before. You're the boss now until I get back to you. If anyone still wants to leave, they have my blessing. I think I have a way to solve the staffing problem."

"There is one other staffing loose end that needs addressed. One of our haulers, guy named Slay Gunther, got involved in a dust up with the state police while on the job. He got busted for reckless driving and resisting arrest. Your father would've probably fired him."

Barlow didn't want to get involved in a personnel matter so soon. "Do you think he should be fired?"

Les paused a beat before responding. "Yes. The guy is a hothead and obnoxious. Not very reliable either."

"Then do it. Fire him. You have my permission."

"That'll leave us short a hauler."

"Like I said, I think I have a way to solve the staffing issue. I'll get back to you."

After slipping into his jacket, Les turned to him and said, "Despite what you might believe, your father wasn't that difficult of a man to work for. I'm being sincere when I tell you I'm going to miss him."

Barlow didn't know what to say.

Les touched the door knob to leave but hesitated. "For what it's worth, your leaving really hurt him. He never let on, but I knew him well enough to tell. It affected him more than when your mother walked out on him."

For the first time in ten years, Barlow felt a twinge of doubt.

9

CHAPTER 9

Petronia's spirits lifted after the rains stopped on Saturday. With the daylight growing shorter in November and the weather turning colder, gloomy skies and rain depressed her. Today, other than pulling over a few speeders on the William Penn Highway and investigating a fender bender in Duncannon, it had been blessedly quiet.

She decided to take her cousin Maggie's advice and go out on her own. When her shift ended, she changed into a red party dress and chose The Inn of the Dancing Bear as her destination. After arriving, she relaxed at one of the tables, drink in hand. It had been a long time since she'd been here, but she remembered how awesome a cook Jill Dunne was, and she had a hankerin' for that woman's famous chili con carne.

She giggled. Words like awesome and hankerin' clued her in that maybe she was drinking too much, too fast, even if she hadn't spoken the words out loud. She was also well-aware of the guys at the bar who had been casting glances her way. A precarious situation. Sooner or later, one of them would work up the nerve to approach her.

Precarious? Yeah, she really needed to slow down. That's another word that didn't usually find its way into her thoughts.

Petronia swished the wine in her glass and studied the overhead fluorescent light reflecting off the red liquid. Checking the time, she noticed it was almost nine. She had arrived at eight, eaten her meal and had what? Three glasses of wine. This was her fourth, but they were small glasses, no more than six ounces. This would be her last, so she decided to nurse it. The band was about to start, and she wanted to sit through their first set. After that, if nobody asked her to dance, she would go home.

Is that really what she wanted? Heck yes. If one of those guys at the bar asked her to dance, she'd take him up on the offer. She liked to dance, and it had been such a long time. Her ex, Charlie, hadn't been much of a dancer.

If a guy approached who seemed sketchy, all she'd need to do would be to flash her wedding ring and show him her badge. That usually deflated a guy more effectively than a cold shower.

While the band tuned up, Petronia pulled an adjacent chair and rested her feet on it, stretching out. She yawned.

Finally, the band started playing. The female lead vocalist who looked to be in her early twenties led off the set with Carrie Underwood's Before He Cheats. The song reminded her of Charlie. The asshole. The girl sang well, sounding exactly like Ms. Underwood. The band wasn't shabby either. The crowd applauded with enthusiasm when the song ended.

After that, the band launched into Fight Song by Rachel Platten. Petronia glanced over at the row of guys sitting at the bar. When was one of them going to ask her?

Wait...she did a double take. Sitting there with his back turned was a man who looked a lot like Barlow Jackson. It couldn't be, could it? She lifted her feet from the chair and sat up straight. She studied the man's reflection in the mirror behind the bar. Oh god, oh god, it was him! Her heart rate accelerated. Of course, he looked older now, and a little world weary, but she'd recognize her first lover and former best friend anywhere.

Or was it just wishful thinking and too much wine? Butterflies floated in her belly.

Barlow!

What was he doing here? How long had he been back in Perry County? Why hadn't he tried contacting her? If he had wanted to find her, he could have. Her mother still lived in the same house.

Was he avoiding her because he had found someone else? She scanned the adjacent bar stools. No woman near him. It hurt her so bad when they had parted; she thought she would die of a broken heart. Why had he insisted on breaking things off so abruptly back then? He had explained how they were on different life paths or some other such nonsense she still couldn't understand. That same hurt from before once again welled in her chest. They had been so close, could finish each other's sentences and read each other's thoughts. Now that he had returned, why hadn't he bothered to find her?

Petronia wanted answers. Needed answers. She should march right up to Barlow and interrogate him like a cop. She took a breath realizing she needed to get control of herself. She downed the rest of her wine. No, she wouldn't approach him as a cop. She'd approach him as the woman he would remember. From her purse, she extracted a vial of perfume and dabbed some on.

Barlow stared into his beer, barely noticing the band had started playing. He had spent the whole day reviewing the company financial records, poring over all the receivables and invoices. He could find nothing irregular. The New Bloomfield housing development project brought in enough cash to make the business robust. As far as he could tell, the company had been legitimately in the black for the past ten years.

Could he have been wrong about his father? The evidence he had found today sure did make him think twice. His father made it clear that times back then were slow, but that was before he left. The contract was awarded a few weeks later, which meant his father hadn't lied about their financial situation.

Ten years ago, his father had been steadfast that there had been no steamer trunk full of cash and the driver had died behind the wheel of the car. But Barlow knew he hadn't hallucinated seeing the steamer trunk and pulling that man from the water.

He couldn't resolve it. If only his father made the effort to contact him to explain? But Barlow probably wouldn't have taken his call. He hadn't been interested in hearing what his father had to say.

Guilt gnawed his insides.

Damn it, if his father hadn't stolen the money and killed that man, then who did?

His subconscious registered the band starting to play one of his favorite tunes, Lady Antebellum's Need You Now. He tried getting the bartender's attention for another beer when from behind, someone reached around and placed hands over his eyes.

He froze, unsure if he should make a defensive move or wait to see what happened next. In his ear, a woman's voice sang softly along with the music.

"And I wonder if I ever cross your mind. For me it happens all the time."

Her mouth was so close that her singing tickled his ear. And she smelled really nice! When she uncovered his eyes, he swiveled on his bar stool to face her.

10

Chapter 10

During the long drive from Columbus, Barlow wondered about the possibility of bumping into Pet, how he would handle it, and what he would say. Here she was, standing right in front of him, smiling, looking mighty fine in a red dress. The way he felt inside made him realize how much he missed her.

"Petronia Henning." He said her name in a steady voice that belied how he felt. His heart raced. "You cut your hair...What are you...How are you..." He couldn't form a complete sentence.

She took his hands. "Shhh. Questions later. Dance with me." She led him onto the small parquet dance floor, joining a half-dozen other couples who swayed in front of the band. She pressed her body against his.

Holding Pet came easy for Barlow; he had done it so often before it was like muscle memory. He knew where all of her curves fit into his, exactly how her head rested against his shoulder, and how she moved to a slow dance.

As if taking a trip back in time, he closed his eyes, relishing every moment until the song ended. When Pet pulled away and squeezed his hand, he felt the ring on her finger.

"I'm by myself at a corner table," she said. "Come. Sit with me."

Barlow followed her, dumbstruck, and they took seats at the table across from each other.

She got the attention of a passing waitress. "Another wine, please. Barlow, what are you drinking?"

He had been drinking beer, but under the circumstances... "Whiskey, please."

Pet raised an eyebrow.

"And a beer chaser."

The waitress walked away. The two of them took each other's measure. Then their gazes met and held.

Barlow broke the silence. "I can't help but to notice you're wearing a ring."

"I can't help but to notice you aren't."

"Yet, you're here by yourself."

"So are you...apparently."

He thought of Caroline. Although they weren't officially exclusive, he didn't want to appear like a loser in front of Pet who obviously was married. "I have a girlfriend...back home...in Ohio."

Pet said nothing.

Barlow glanced at the bar. Where was that waitress? "Do I know your husband? Did he go to school with us?"

"He grew up in Dauphin County. You probably don't know him."

"Where are you living now?"

"I have an apartment outside of Newport."

"Your parents, uh, do they still live at the same place?" He had seen the name on the mailbox and figured they did.

She nodded. "My dad passed. Mom still lives at the house."

"Oh, sorry about your father."

The waitress returned with their drinks. Barlow downed his shot of whiskey and took a drink from his beer mug.

Pet fingered the stem of her wineglass but held off on drinking. "Am I making you uncomfortable?"

More like breathless. Overcome with emotion seeing her. Realizing how much he missed her. "No, of course not." Wanting to change the subject, he added, "My father also died."

The news seemed to stun her. She pressed her lips together for a moment before resuming her pleasant expression. "I didn't know. When did it happen?"

"A few days ago. It's the reason why I'm back. To settle his estate."

"I see." She took a sip of wine and wore a blank expression.

What was she thinking? Did she miss him as much as he missed her? Of course, not. She was married. "What does your husband do?"

"He's a financial advisor. What do you do?"

"I work in construction. And you?"

She hesitated. "Look, the song is over, but we're still dancing. Let's lay our cards on the table. Why, Barlow? Why wouldn't you ever answer my email, texts, or take my calls after you left?"

Barlow feared it would come to this. He hung his head. "Pet, it was better that I didn't."

"Why?"

He did it for her, so she could move on. He wouldn't have been good enough for her. Barlow looked up, met her gaze. "I had my reasons."

She raised her voice. "If it weren't for your mother telling me news about you, I would have thought you had been killed over there in that hellhole of a country where you were stationed."

Barlow's gut churned. "Pet, breaking up hurt me too."

"It hurt you? What about me, Barlow? Did you even take my feelings into consideration? Did you think that maybe I had a say in whether or not we had a future together?"

Barlow sighed. "I'm sorry, Pet. There are no other words. I'm just so sorry."

Pet downed the rest of her wine. "I used to play it in my head what I would say if we ever met again. I should be angry with you, but I'm not. I can't."

Barlow laid his arm on the table, hand open, inviting her to take his. "I'm glad you don't hate me, Pet. You still have a special place in my heart. You always will." No mere words, he felt it, and he needed to say it.

She regarded his hand but didn't take it. She scoffed and stood. "I should go."

"I wish you would stay a while." It felt as if they were breaking up all over again.

Pet didn't meet his gaze. She gripped the back of her chair. "I need to get home."

"To your husband?"

She said nothing.

"You look fantastic, Pet, as beautiful as I remember you. Actually, more beautiful."

She held her arms out at her side, as if saying, look at me. "And yet...you threw me away."

Her words felt like a punch to the gut. "That's not fair. It wasn't like that."

She shook her head and turned to leave.

"Wait," Barlow blurted.

She placed a hand on her hip and eyed him.

He felt ridiculous and pathetic. "Do you think? I don't know, it might be nice to talk again sometime."

"What exactly are you asking me, Barlow?"

"Can I have your number?"

"Now? Ten years of silence, and now you want my number?"

"C'mon, Pet, don't bust my balls."

One corner of her mouth turned up into a smile. "When we were teens, you used to complain all the time about me busting your balls."

"Yeah? Well, you're still good at it."

She took some time considering. "All right, I'll give you my card, but given our history, I won't hold my breath over ever hearing from you again." She reached into her clutch and pulled out a business card, laid it face down on the tabletop, and left him.

He watched Pet thread her way through the crowd and between the tables. When she reached the door, she turned to look back but didn't wave before walking out.

Barlow picked up the card and turned it over. A Commonwealth of Pennsylvania insignia. Below her name, he read her title, Trooper, Pennsylvania State Police.

"Wow!" he uttered. "How did that happen?"

11

CHAPTER 11

Petronia knew she was impaired while driving home, that last glass of wine having tipped her over the edge. She drove the speed limit and fortunately was able to keep her car between the lines. Drinking so much had been reckless and irresponsible of her. She thought about the nightmare scenario of being pulled over by one of her colleagues, being administered a sobriety test, and arrested.

It would be humiliating and likely end her career in law enforcement.

"I'm not going to try to excuse my behavior, but a perfect storm of circumstances caused me to overindulge." She slapped the side of her face. "I'm more than a little impaired if I'm talking to myself."

Petronia's emotions swirled as she replayed the conversation with Barlow in her head. She had gotten over him a long time ago, right? So why did her heart ache now that she had seen him again? Why did she wish things had turned out differently?

She felt the same hurt now she had ten years ago when they had parted. She never understood his reason. She thought he had loved her more than anything in the world and had expected Barlow to ask her to marry him. Sure, it would've been difficult. They would've had to make a home while she attended university and while he was overseas, but they could've survived. Other couples did it. Why hadn't he wanted to at least try?

Reality washed over her as she pulled into her driveway. This was her life now, working odd hours as a state trooper, and an ex-husband she had settled for.

Settled for. She let that thought hang.

Why hadn't she told Barlow about her divorce? Because it was none of his goddamn business, that's why. Let him think she was married. Let him envy what he had missed out on.

Oh, she was really drunk and emotionally spent. Her head spun and her stomach felt queasy. She unlocked the door to her apartment and her already queasy stomach roiled. She ran for the bathroom to the toilet bowl and tossed up the chili she had enjoyed earlier.

When the wave of nausea ended, she washed her face. While rinsing with mouthwash, she glanced in the mirror. "Barlow has my nerves and emotions in a knot. That's probably contributed to my feeling sick."

Barlow told her he had a girlfriend. He had obviously moved on. Here she was a divorced loser who hadn't had the guts to tell him she was no longer married.

Pathetic. If only she could replay the night over again.

She shuffled to her bedroom and peeled off her clothes, somehow managed to struggle into her flannel pajamas, and sulked.

"I still love you, Barlow," she whispered.

She had way too much to drink. Tomorrow she would pay the price.

Pay the price.

Pay.

"Oh, no!" Petronia shrieked and brought both fists to her mouth. She had been so tipsy and distracted by her encounter with Barlow that she had walked out of the Dancing Bear having forgotten to pay her bill.

She felt mortified. Trevor and Jill Dunne, the owners of the inn knew her and also knew she was in law enforcement. What would they think of her?

Grabbing her phone, she dialed directory assistance and asked for the Dancing Bear's number.

After getting the number from the operator, she dialed right away. On the third ring, a man answered, practically shouting into the phone, "Inn of the Dancing Bear, this is Anson."

She knew Anson was one of the bartenders. She could hear the band playing in the background. "This is Petronia Henning. Look, I'm so embarrassed. I was there tonight but forgot to pay my bill before leaving."

"What?" Anson yelled. "You're going to have to speak up to be heard over the band."

Great. Her head was pounding and the last thing she wanted to do was to scream into a phone. She cupped her hand over the receiver and repeated what she had just told him.

After a pause at the other end of the line, Anson said, "Sure, Trooper Henning, I know who you are."

"I'll stop by tomorrow and settle my bill."

"Hang on," Anson said. She heard the thump of the receiver as he laid it on the bar.

What was he doing? Why did he put the phone down?

He came back on the line. "I just spoke with your waitress. The gentleman you were with took care of your bill."

Petronia squeezed shut her eyes. The gentleman she was with.

"Are you still there?" Anson asked.

"Yes. Thank you. I'm sorry, and it won't happen again."

"No problem," he said before ending the call.

Barlow had rescued her. Just like he always did when they were growing up. If he had a girlfriend, why had he asked for her number? How serious was his relationship with his girlfriend? How long would it take to settle his father's estate? How long would he be in Perry County?

Petronia groaned. What did any of it matter? He wouldn't call, and she had no way of finding him or getting in touch. She would never see him again.

Still, there was hope. He had asked for her number.

Regret gripped her chest. Why hadn't she asked Barlow for his?

12

Chapter 12

The next morning, Barlow left his room and walked downstairs to the restaurant for breakfast. He chose to sit at the same table he and Pet had occupied the night before. Maybe it was his imagination, but he thought her scent still lingered mixed in with the miasma of stale beer.

He hadn't slept well after his conversation with her. She seemed happy with her life and married.

He felt miserable. It would've been better had their paths not crossed last night. Now, he couldn't stop obsessing about her and about what could have been had they stayed together. What had seemed the right thing to do back then, now in hindsight, may have been the biggest mistake of his life. He still loved her. He had never stopped loving her.

While lying in bed last night staring up at the ceiling, Barlow pondered her career choice as a state trooper. Maybe she could help him resolve the mystery surrounding his father? Maybe he was just looking for a reason to contact her again. Except, she was married. Why should he torture himself?

Considering the possibility his father might have been telling the truth, he wondered, could he spend some time researching the incident on his own? If he could discover any information that would settle his doubt one way or another over his father's involvement, it would ease his mind. Finding such information would be a long shot after so many years.

Barlow finished his breakfast and signaled for the waitress. When she approached, he asked, "Do you know if there's a library around here?"

"We have local libraries, but they aren't open Sundays. What exactly do you want to research?"

"I was hoping to look at old newspaper archives."

"Don't need a library for that," she said, "the Harrisburg newspaper covers Perry County. You can search their archives online."

Great idea. "Where can I find a computer around here?"

She shrugged. "You might ask the boss if you can use the office computer."

"Can you get the boss for me?" He handed her a ten-dollar tip.

She gawked at the ten and smiled. "Thanks, mister. Wait here."

A few minutes later, a raven-haired woman in her thirties emerged from the kitchen. She marched up to him and asked, "Can I help you?"

He was under the impression Trevor was the boss. "Is Trevor working today?"

"He'll be in later. I'm Jill, Trevor's wife."

"This may seem like an odd request, but..." Barlow explained to her his need to use a computer and asked if one might be available.

Jill looked at him with a stoic expression. "You're right. That is an odd request. As far as I know, nobody has ever asked to use our computer before."

"I wouldn't be asking except there's something important I need to research. Out here in the country, I just don't where else to go to."

She ran a hand through her hair. "I don't know. I'd have to let you sit in our office where we keep all our business records. I can't chaperone you because I'm busy preparing for the Sunday brunch crowd."

"I promise you, I have no interest in snooping around in your business. My eyes will remain locked on the computer screen."

She stood there considering it.

Barlow said, "I don't mind if you charge me extra for the service."

"Since you have a room here, we have your driver's license and credit card on file. We can track you down if anything goes missing or is found out of place." She said it with a smile, but Barlow understood the underlying threat.

"I appreciate it and promise I won't take long."

Jill led him into the back of the inn to a small office. She powered up the computer, logged on, and told him to sit. "Gotta get back to the kitchen," she said before scampering away.

Beside the keyboard, Barlow noticed a family photo. Trevor, Jill, and two kids he assumed to be theirs. One of the kids, a boy in his mid-teens, and the other a girl of around eight. He reminded himself he had promised to not snoop around and turned his attention to the computer.

He pulled up the Harrisburg newspaper web site and typed in: "Perry County car crash" and the date from ten years ago.

It surprised him how many hits were returned. He scrolled for a few minutes until finding the right article. The headline read: College Student Drowns.

State police in Newport investigated the scene of a fatal crash outside of Millerstown where a sedan driven by Neil Mantener, 22, of Lewistown was found submerged in the Juniata River during the early morning hours of August 15. Investigators determined that Mantener had been driving at a high rate of speed and failed to negotiate a curve whereby he left the roadway and plunged into the river. He was found dead at the scene. The coroner determined the cause of death to be drowning.

Mantener's family could not explain what he was doing in that area of the commonwealth and at that hour. A senior at Penn State University majoring in electrical engineering, he was last seen in his room during the day prior to his death. Mantener's friends and associates reported him to be in good spirits and could offer no further explanation as to his behavior. As far as the investigators could determine, he had no ties in Perry County.

Barlow considered what he had just read. It seemed so perfunctory. A man had died, nobody could offer an explanation, and that was the end of the story. No mention of a steamer trunk full of cash.

He did another search but could find no other follow up articles. What about all the unanswered questions? Wasn't anybody curious enough to dig deeper? If not the police, then why not the newspaper reporters?

He knew nothing more than before and resigned himself that he never would know what happened to the cash or how the man ended up back in his car. He'd never know for sure whether his father had been involved, although he now suspected his father had not been.

Wanting to honor his promise to Jill to leave her office as soon as possible, Barlow clicked on the menu to bring up the power off icon. Just then, he noticed an article following the one he had read:

Police have no suspects or leads in the mysterious Harrisburg Convention Center robbery. A large amount of cash is still missing. Story continues on page D3.

13

CHAPTER 13

Barlow finished studying the newspaper archives, and as far as he could determine, the theft at the convention center taking place during the Summer National Sports and Outdoor Show had never been solved. From the sketchy information found in the news articles, someone had entered the vault during the busiest day of the summer show, one of the largest, most well-attended in the country, and made off with a lot of cash.

The gate and parking money were held in the vault with the cash scheduled to be picked up by an armored car service early the next morning. The quantity of money stolen wasn't disclosed, although one unnamed source speculated the amount to be well into six figures.

Barlow calculated the robbery occurred about four hours before the incident with the submerged car. The amount of cash would've been consistent with what he had seen in the trunk, and Harrisburg was located across the river only about an hour away.

Had the driver, Neil Mantener, been the perpetrator? If so, it still didn't answer what had happened to the money and who had drowned the man and moved him back into the car.

Why didn't the police make the connection between Mantener and the robbery? Then again, with no cash at the scene of the accident, why should they? They would see the accident as a random event caused by a university student driving too fast on an unknown road.

Barlow digested the information and decided he would call Pet and let her know what happened. She had access to information that might not be readily available to the general public.

Would Pet think he had an ulterior motive for calling? Did he? He pulled his phone and the business card she had given him the night before. Would she think this to be a cheesy excuse, something he invented to talk to her again. He reminded himself that she was married.

He reconsidered. "It's not as if I'm asking her out. This really is a matter for the police." He punched in her number.

She picked up on the second ring. "Trooper Petronia Henning speaking."

"Pet, um, this is Barlow."

"So, you decided to call? I gotta say I'm surprised, but Barlow, I'm on duty right now. Can I call you back in a few minutes?" She sounded genuinely happy to hear from him.

"I just want to ask if we can meet later after you get off."

"You sound tense. Are you okay?"

"I'm fine. Instead of calling me back we should meet. What I have to tell you is complicated."

She giggled. "My life is full of complications. I don't want any more."

"I need your help as a law enforcement officer. Official business."

With an amused tone, she said, "If you got a speeding ticket, I can't do anything about it."

"Pet, listen to me. It has to do with the night we broke up and about that freak accident."

"You mean when that guy drove his car into the river and drowned?"

"Yeah. I found out something about the accident today that I hadn't known before."

"Hmm. You've piqued my curiosity. When and where do you want to meet?"

"The Dancing Bear at seven. Does that work for you?"

"Why there? I assumed you were staying at your dad's old house?"

Too many bad vibes at that place. He was happy with his decision to stay at the inn. "I have a room here. We can talk in my room or at the bar if you prefer."

"I'm done at six. I should be able to meet you around seven."

He noted how she hadn't balked at meeting him in his room. "I'd appreciate if you came alone."

"What's that supposed to mean?" Her tone took on a suspicious edge. Maybe he had assumed too much. Maybe she wanted to bring Charlie.

"Someday I want to meet your husband." Yeah, when hell froze over. "But not tonight. What I have to tell you about that incident is weird, so I'd like to keep it confidential for now. Between you and me."

She considered his request and agreed. Barlow ended the call. Husband or not, his heart beat a little faster in anticipation of seeing her again.

Petronia arrived early and didn't see Barlow at the bar. She thought about ordering a drink while waiting but decided instead to find him. She got the attention of Anson, the bartender, and asked which room Barlow was staying in.

"That guy you were with last night?"

She scoffed. "I was not with him. He's an old friend who asked me to stop by tonight to inform me about something that's official police business."

Anson laughed. "In his room? What kind of police business would that be?"

"Police business that's none of your business."

Anson leaned with both hands on the bar. "You have a warrant?" The smile on his face signaled he was just messing with her.

She smiled back at him. "No, but during some busy evening I could park my cruiser outside your door. I wonder what effect that would have on business? I'm sure you would like to explain that to your boss."

Anson raised his hands in mock surrender. "Room seven."

Petronia walked up the stairs, found room seven, and knocked.

Barlow opened and greeted her, his eyes settling on the gap in her V-neck sweater. It was tight and exposed a little too much of her, but she had chosen it on purpose to remind him what he had given up.

"Let's talk downstairs in the dining room," Barlow said. "I could use a drink."

"Me too," Petronia said, although she felt a bit disappointed losing the intimacy of meeting in his room.

They chose a corner table farthest from the bar.

Barlow motioned for Anson. The man sauntered over, a look of annoyance on his face. "Why such a faraway table? You want to make sure I get my exercise tonight or what?"

As far as Petronia was concerned, the guy just lost a few percentage points off his tip.

"We need privacy," Barlow explained.

"Yeah, right," Anson said in a flat tone while tapping a pencil against his pad. "Official police business. What'll you have?"

They both ordered draft beer. After last night, Petronia couldn't stomach anything stronger. She would nurse her one drink. Or maybe she'd have two.

Since it was a slow night, it took only a minute for Anson to return with the drafts. When he left, Barlow took a long pull and ran a sleeve across his lips. He looked her in the eye. "I'm hoping we can pick up on our conversation we started last night."

Petronia felt the same way, but she didn't want to appear too eager. "I thought this meeting was about some information you wanted to share."

"It is. Let me start by telling you about my walk home during our final night together."

The story he told about the steamer trunk full of cash and a man he had saved from drowning contradicted everything Pet knew about that accident. What he said seemed hard to believe but given their history, she knew Barlow well. He wasn't the kind of man to make up fantastic stories.

In the back of her mind, she had to wonder. Why was he telling her all these things now?

14

CHAPTER 14

Barlow hadn't realized how much of a weight it had been carrying his secret. Telling his story to Pet left him feeling unburdened. She was so easy to talk to, just like back then. She was also so easy to look at, just like back then.

Pet motioned Anson over to order a second round of drinks. She sat up straight in her chair. His story had obviously gotten her attention and interest.

"Let me get this straight," she said. "For the past decade you suspected your father might be a murderer?"

"At the time, what else could I think? What other possible explanation could there be?"

"My god, Barlow, that's insane! Your dad was a hard ass, but I never believed him to be capable of murder."

"I wasn't hallucinating that night, and you and I weren't exactly partying. We were stone cold sober when we broke up. It happened exactly like I told you."

"Just to clarify. We didn't break up. You broke up with me."

"There you go, busting my balls again."

She waved him off. "Anyway, you wrote your father out of your life over what might be a misunderstanding. That is so profoundly sad and tragic."

No...letting Pet go had been sad and tragic. Now, it was too late.

She leaned forward across the table. "Why didn't you tell me all of this back then?"

"I didn't know how desperate Dad might be. If you talked, and he found out about it, I didn't know what he might do. If he killed that man, he might..." Barlow didn't finish.

"Your father isn't a killer, and now you're jumping to conclusions over a possible unrelated newspaper story."

"I reviewed my father's books from his business and interviewed his foreman. I'm realizing now that Dad came into a lot of money legitimately around that time."

Pet said nothing for a few moments while staring at her beer mug. "How do you think I can help you?"

"You have access to police reports. Can you look at both incidents, the car crash and the robbery? Knowing what I told you, maybe you can find a connection."

She went silent while considering his request. "Obviously, that case happened way before my joining the PSP. I suppose I could talk my supervisor into letting me look into it on my own time as a hobby case."

Barlow sipped his beer. "A hobby case?"

"That's what we call it. Working on old cases after hours, you know, like a hobby." She grew pensive. "If something comes of this, you would be expected to make an official statement." She looked directly at him. "Are you willing to commit to that eventuality?"

"If it becomes necessary, I'll go on the record. In the meantime, why don't you find some way to take a quick look. See if you can find anything substantial."

Pet took another swallow from her beer and set down her mug.

Barlow couldn't help himself. His eyes wandered to the vee of her sweater. Pleasant memories of her breasts pressed against his bare chest invaded his thoughts.

She caught him looking but didn't say anything. Did she still carry the same pleasant memories of their time together?

"I have to know the truth about my father. You can understand that, right?"

Pet nodded. "I'll see what I can do, but no promises that I'll be able to find anything. There may be nothing to connect the two incidents."

"That's all I can ask. How long will it take you?"

She leaned forward, a gleam in her eye. "How long will you be in Perry County?"

Barlow considered how long he might be able to stay. "I planned to return to Ohio tomorrow morning. My boss really needs me to finish laying shingles before it snows."

"This is Thanksgiving week. How about I call after the holidays on Monday a week from tomorrow to give you an update."

"That's fine. Let me give you my number."

She flashed a shy smile. "I already saved it from when you called me earlier today."

It gave him a warm feeling, her saving his number, but he reminded himself not to read too much into it. "Text me or call if you find out anything sooner."

"Of course."

She pulled a twenty from her purse and set it on the table.

"Put that away. I got it."

"Nothing doing. You paid last night. Oh, and I'm sorry about that. I didn't mean to stick you with the bill. The shock of seeing you, I guess, distracted me."

"It's nice to know I can still distract you. Speaking of distractions, I gotta say you rock that outfit you're wearing."

He noticed how she tried suppressing a smile. "Are you hitting on me?"

Of course, he was. "Me? Hitting on a married woman?"

She stiffened, took a deep breath, and acted as if she was about to say something. But she went quiet.

"What's wrong, Pet?"

"You told me you have a girlfriend. What are you going to tell her about spending time with your ex?"

Nothing. Why should he? He shrugged and said nothing.

"My woman's intuition senses the two of you aren't very serious. You haven't even told me her name. You don't talk about her."

"Caroline isn't here right now. I'm with you. Right now that's all that matters."

Pet's gaze went to her lap. When she looked up, Barlow saw her cheeks had turned rosy. "You're flirting with me. Just how serious are you and Caroline?"

He and Caroline were on the verge of becoming exclusive. "Serious enough." Except his rekindled feelings for Pet confused him. If only she weren't married..."Enough about me. Tell me about your husband. How did the two of you meet?"

She paused a long time before answering and scrutinized him. Barlow wondered why. "It's not such a special story. The two of us met at university, started dating, and got engaged shortly after graduation."

"How did you end up becoming a state trooper?"

"My degrees are in criminal justice and forensics. I dreamed of working for the FBI but ended up here...because Charlie got a job in Harrisburg."

He detected resentment in her tone. "I take it Charlie isn't supportive of your career path?"

Pet scoffed. "That's putting it mildly. He didn't even want me to work." She covered her mouth as if she misspoke. "I mean he doesn't want me to work. Tells me he makes enough money so I can stay at home." She dropped her hand to the tabletop. "It's like he expects me to waste my life doing nothing."

Without thinking, Barlow reached over and laid his hand on top of hers. Growing up they had always held hands. If felt as natural as breathing.

Pet's gaze drifted to their now-entwined fingers. Then she met his gaze. "I can't stay much longer. I'm back on duty at six tomorrow morning."

Barlow swallowed. Her hand in his felt so right. "I'm really happy we had a chance to reconnect."

Pet squeezed shut her eyes as if in pain and slowly slid her hand away. "You have a girlfriend, Barlow."

"I'm sorry, Pet. I shouldn't have done that."

"It's okay, and I really should go."

"Are we good?"

"Yeah, we're good. Don't worry about it." She stood. "Since I caught you up with my life, it's only fair that next time you tell me all about yourself. I want to hear about your time in the military, your life in Ohio...and more about Caroline."

"I can't wait to see you again." Barlow felt elated there would be a next time.

15

CHAPTER 15

Sitting at her desk at the Newport state police barracks, Petronia had trouble concentrating. She had dreams and ambitions that her ex-husband Charlie never could accept. After college he had quickly found a job in Harrisburg. With his degree in finance and MBA, the man seemed stable, solid, and sensible. A firm foundation for raising a family.

She never hid her desire about wanting a career in law enforcement. Charlie asked her to marry him clearly knowing what she wanted. He was supportive when she had applied to the state police academy. Petronia wondered now whether he had assumed she would wash out because of being a woman.

On the job now for four years as a trooper, she hoped someday to become a detective. Breaking a cold case murder could earn her that opportunity. She wasn't working this hobby case just for Barlow.

Petronia tried picturing what her life would be like had she married Barlow. There was never a time during her childhood and teen years where he wasn't protective of her. A girl couldn't ask for a finer friend. Or lover. Soul mates was an overused cliché, yet that's what they had been back then. Maybe they still were?

Which is why she felt so abandoned after he had ghosted on her. Was she being a fool sticking her neck out again for a man who had deserted her once before?

A few of her fellow colleagues milled around the station, but most of the troopers on her shift had already taken to the road. She was waiting to see her barracks commander, Lieutenant Jardine. He sat in his office on the phone behind a wall of glass. She waited until he hung up before approaching and knocking.

The man motioned for her to enter. "Are you here to discuss that dirt bag, Slay Gunther?"

Pet took a seat in the visitor chair across the desk from him. "No. That's water under the bridge."

"Just so you know, the DA informed me he read your report and is taking your side. He wants to see the man do jail time over the way he behaved during your encounter with him."

"Wouldn't break my heart," Petronia said, "but I want to ask you about something else."

The lieutenant raised an eyebrow.

She cleared her throat. "There's a hobby case I'd like to pursue." She went on to tell the lieutenant how an informant tipped her to some new information about an old, unsolved case, but she didn't reveal any details. She finished by reminding him of her goal to someday become a detective. The hobby case would be good experience for her.

"I can't see the harm in it," he said, "if you pursue it on your own time."

She stood. "Will do, LT."

"And loop me in if you discover anything actionable."

That evening, after her shift, Petronia sat at a computer terminal to begin her research.

"Ten years ago," she mumbled. Finding the report about the car accident didn't take long. She remembered that day, the police cars in front of her house and the ambulance. Nothing appeared in the case file she hadn't already known. Neil Mantener, 22, drove his car at a high rate of speed and ended up in the Juniata River. The coroner pronounced him dead due to drowning. Simple as that. No mention of any money. Interviews with family and friends provided no explanation as to what Mantener was doing in Perry County at that hour of morning.

A bit of a mystery perhaps, but nothing that would warrant a follow up. From experience, she knew most of the time there was no explanation as to why people did the crazy things they did to get into trouble.

Finding information about the convention center robbery was trickier. That case had been handled by the Harrisburg barracks. She would be able to locate digital records, but any physical evidence would be located off site, and she would have to make an official request to access it.

Petronia entered the year of the incident and search terms: Harrisburg Convention Center and Summer National Sports and Outdoor Show.

Her computer display listed a date, case number, and name of the detective assigned to the case, a man named Custer Graham. She didn't know Custer Graham and had never heard of him. She opened the computer file to access the details. Ordinarily, a robbery investigation, especially one of this magnitude, would generate hundreds of pages detailing timelines, evidence, and interviews.

The file contained only one page with one typed line. It read: Administratively Closed.

"What the hell?" She stared at the screen. Administratively Closed? What did that mean? She had never run across anything like it before.

Morg Johansson, a trooper first class who worked night duty entered the barracks. He was a big man with a solid build. Morg once joked with her how he had descended from a long line of Swedish lumberjacks. A decent guy. Having been a trooper for fifteen years, he could've opted for day shift or moved up the chain of command. He was a loner who preferred working nights and on patrol.

"Hey, Morg, can I bother you a minute?"

The man smiled and approached. He towered over Petronia while she remained seated at the computer. "Talking with you is never a bother. What's up?"

"Did you ever run across a police report tagged with the phrase, administratively closed?"

Morg's eyes went wide, and he sucked in a breath. "What have you gotten yourself into, Trooper Henning?"

Surprised at the way her question had unnerved him, she worried she might have stumbled onto something unauthorized. Before she could explain, Morg gently laid a hand on her shoulder. He glanced around the barracks as if concerned someone might overhear their conversation. In a low voice, he said, "Whatever you're researching, drop it. Forget you saw what you saw."

"You can't just leave me hanging with a statement like that. What gives, Morg?"

"Administratively closed is a euphemism meaning the case has been deemed too sensitive to maintain in the police database."

"I get it. Hardcopy only, probably kept in an office safe somewhere." She knew there was little chance she'd be able to gain access to the case file. Barlow was going to be disappointed, and she would need a different case to prove her detective skills.

Morg shook his head. "No, you don't get it. Administratively closed means that no digital data exists, no hardcopy, no evidence whatsoever. The public is told the investigation is ongoing, but in reality, the case is spiked."

She went quiet and tried wrapping her mind around his words.

He took another look around before saying, "It takes someone way, way up the food chain to stop an investigation, a person with powerful political connections."

Stunned, she said, "Maybe I'm naïve, but are you telling me there are people who are above the law, people who wield enough clout they can order the Pennsylvania State Police to stand down from an active investigation? That's unbelievable."

Morg leaned in inches from her face. "Here's what you'd better believe. Continue poking around an administratively closed case, and you'll likely be fired. Or worse."

16

Chapter 16

Barlow was awakened by the rustle of covers and Caroline's warm body spooned against his back. Her arm reached around him, and her hand came to rest against his belly. He opened one eye to check the time. The digital alarm clock on his nightstand read 5:14.

He would soon have to get up and go to work. The wind rattled the windows of his apartment. It would be a cold day laying shingles. He was tempted to bask in Caroline's warmth a little longer.

While making the eight-hour drive back from Pennsylvania, Barlow had grown despondent. Seeing Pet should have provided him with some sort of closure. She was married, happy, and had moved on with her life. Isn't that what he had wanted for her? Wasn't that his motive for breaking up with her in the first place?

If so, why did he feel such regret? So empty inside? Why had he driven to The Eight Ball and thrown himself at Caroline, keeping her company until closing and then inviting her back to his place?

He felt guilty taking advantage of her, all the while thinking about Pet, wishing he was with Pet. It wasn't the first time he and Caroline had sex, but under the circumstances, sleeping with her last night had been wrong. Caroline was a sweet, nurturing young lady. She didn't deserve to be used as an object to satisfy his sexual longing.

Barlow carefully untangled himself, trying not to disturb her sleep, and headed for the bathroom. After stumbling through his morning shave and shower ritual, he exited the bathroom and found the bed empty. "Caroline?"

From down the hall, he heard her voice. "I'm in the kitchen."

He slipped into his work clothes and detected the pleasing aroma of bacon frying. Barlow found her at the stove, barefoot, wearing nothing but one of his flannel shirts. He did have feelings for her, it was just that...

She wasn't Pet.

He hugged her from behind. "I wish you wouldn't sacrifice your sleep to make me breakfast."

She giggled. "Is that your way of saying you don't like my cooking?"

"You know that's not true."

"Don't worry. After you leave, I'm going back to bed and sleep until noon." She paused to flip the eggs in the fry pan.

Barlow took a seat at the table.

She set a plate in front of him. Two eggs over easy, toasted wheat bread, and six strips of bacon. His favorite breakfast combo. She poured a glass of orange juice for him and started the coffee.

Guilt dampened his appetite, but he wanted to show his appreciation. He forked eggs into his mouth. "You're too good to me. You spoil me."

"That's the general idea." She sat across the table and watched him eat. "I'm not going to have breakfast yet, because it'll keep me from getting back to sleep." She regarded him. "Barlow, I'm sorry about your dad. Did you get everything squared away while in Pennsylvania?"

He set down his fork. "No. I'm going to have to go back after Thanksgiving to finish up."

Caroline ran her fingers through her long, thick mane of gorgeous hair. "I worry about you. You didn't seem yourself last night. Distant." She took a breath. "I know you served. If it's PTSD from your time deployed with the Marines, that's okay and it won't scare me off, but you should tell me about it so I can understand when you get this way."

Crap. She had noticed he had been distracted. Her words made him feel even more guilty. She was sweet and accommodating. She always tried so hard to please him. "It's not PTSD. I was deployed over there, but my unit was tasked with guarding sensitive military facilities. Other than a few half-hearted attacks by hostiles, I never had to engage in prolonged combat."

His words seemed to mollify her. He picked up his fork meaning to finish off his eggs.

She watched him eat. "Now that we've been together for a while, I was wondering if I should give up my place and move in with you."

Why now? Why did she ask him this now when he was so damn confused?

When he didn't answer, Caroline rested a hand against her chest. "Am I moving too fast, assuming too much?"

Barlow rubbed his forehead. "Hear me out. During the past ten years I may have deluded myself into believing a lie about my father." He hadn't directly answered her question and wondered if he was making sense. "Look, do you really want me to unload all of this onto you?"

She smiled. "I'm a professional waitress and bartender. People unload their troubles onto me all day long. I'm probably better at listening than most therapists, so go ahead, lay it on me."

He told her the whole story, but left out all the parts about Pet. While he spoke, the coffee finished brewing and Caroline poured them each a cup. When done, Barlow realized he still hadn't answered her question. He didn't know how to answer it. Pet was married, out of his reach, and Caroline was an awesome lady who cared for him. He sipped his coffee, stalling for time.

She drummed her fingers against the tabletop. "Are you just going to let things go, or are you going to try to find out what really happened that long ago night?"

"I'm working on it."

She cocked her head. "How?"

"I have an old friend who happens to be a state trooper. This trooper friend of mine is making some inquiries and doing some research for me."

Caroline perked up. "That's really cool. When is he going to get back to you?"

He. The word hung in the air. Caroline had backed him into a corner, but he wasn't going to lie to her. Barlow cleared his throat. "She."

"What?"

"My trooper friend is a she. Her name is Petronia. We grew up together. I've known her for almost my entire life. That's why she agreed to help me."

Caroline took a long drink from her coffee. His confession didn't seem to bother her. She took it in stride. "When is she going to get back to you?"

"Pet is going to call me Monday after this Thanksgiving weekend."

Caroline set down her coffee cup. "Pet? You call her Pet?"

Oh, crap. "It's just a nickname from when we were kids."

"Uh, huh, when Pet calls you with the details of her investigation, is that when you'll return to Pennsylvania?"

Barlow shrugged. "Yeah, I'll need to go over things with her."

"And it isn't something you could simply do over the phone?"

She had a point, but he didn't want to talk to her over the phone. He yearned to see her again, in the flesh. "I don't think so. By the way, Petronia is married."

"Good for her."

He wondered if she would let it drop.

"So, about me moving in?"

If it hadn't been for his rekindled feelings for Pet, Barlow would be filled with joy over Caroline's willingness to commit to him. What was wrong with him? He and Pet were over. Finished. In the past. He had left her and then lost her to another man. Why wasn't he encouraging Caroline and heartily agreeing that she should move in?

Caroline hung her head. "Your silence speaks volumes."

"It's not you. It's me," Barlow mumbled.

She groaned. "That is such a cliché. Why don't you just tell me you don't want me to move in with you?"

"Give me a break, Caroline. My head isn't in the right place having to deal with my father's situation." And dealing with his inappropriate feelings for Pet.

Caroline met Barlow's gaze. He saw compassion in her eyes. She said, "I'm sorry. You're right. Your father just died, and I'm being insensitive. Now's not the right time."

Barlow hoped he would be able to put his feelings for Pet behind him and someday soon he and Caroline could take that next step. "I'll work it out, I promise." When though? When would he get over his confused mess of emotions?

Caroline stood. "I'm going back to bed. I'll be gone before you return from work this afternoon."

"You don't have to—"

"—Yeah, I do. Oh, and Barlow, when you return to Pennsylvania, I'm coming with you."

17

Chapter 17

After Petronia completed her shift, she sat at her desk at the state police barracks and fired up her computer. It had been a long day, not from anything that happened while she was on patrol, but from thoughts swirling in her head.

The words: administratively closed, continued to invade her thoughts along with Morg Johansson's threat of her possibly being fired if she poked around in the Harrisburg convention center robbery. It grated on her sensibilities how investigation of a felony could be roadblocked due to politics. Someone was being protected. Who? What gave them the right to consider themselves above the law?

The whole situation didn't sit well with her.

Petronia stared at her computer screen. The only information provided in the case file was the name she had previously noticed, that of lead investigator Detective Custer Graham, the man she had never heard of. Since striving to become a detective, she was familiar with the hierarchy. Both the state police and state attorney general office had bureaus of criminal investigation. Detectives from the AG office specialized in narcotics investigations.

Was that why she wasn't familiar with Detective Graham? Did he work for the AG? If so, how were drugs involved with the Harrisburg convention center robbery or with the young man, Neil Mantener, crashing his car into the river?

She should just let it go.

She should, but she couldn't. Petronia picked up her desk phone and dialed the main number for Troop H headquarters in Harrisburg. When the receptionist answered, she identified herself and asked if Detective Graham worked in her office.

"I've been here less than a year," the receptionist told her. "Let me transfer you to one of the sergeants in personnel."

A few moments later, a gruff male voice picked up and identified himself as Sergeant Tanzin.

Petronia introduced herself again and stated the purpose of her call.

"Yeah, I know Custer Graham. A good detective. He retired about eight years ago."

That explained why she had never run into him before. He had been before her time with the PSP. "I'm working on an old, unsolved case of his. Can you give me his home phone number? I have some questions he might be able to clear up for me."

The line went silent. "Hello?"

The sergeant cleared his throat. "Who did you say you were again?"

She repeated her name and badge number. "Is there a problem?"

"We don't normally give out that information over the phone. You'll have to go through channels."

Petronia wouldn't want her phone number given out either, but she had hoped he could make an exception. "What's the procedure to go through official channels?"

"Have your barracks commander submit the request in writing on PSP letterhead."

"I don't have time for that." Her words came out harsher than she wanted. "I apologize. It's been a long day."

"I understand," Sergeant Tanzin said, his voice friendly and sympathetic. "Custer was a thorough detective and kept meticulous case files. If there's anything you need to know, I'm sure you'll find it in his files."

Petronia took a breath. "I really need to talk to him."

"Maybe I can help. What's the name of the open case you're working?"

She almost told him before remembering Morg Johansson's warning words: "Continue poking around an administratively closed case, and you'll likely be fired. Or worse."

"I have another call coming in that I have to take," she lied. "Thanks for your time. I'll submit my request through channels as you instructed." She ended the call, realizing she needed to find another way to track the man down.

On a whim, she found phone books for the three surrounding counties: Dauphin, Cumberland, and Perry. Since the detective worked out of Harrisburg, it seemed likely he lived in the area, that is, if he hadn't moved away. It didn't surprise Petronia when she found no listing for Custer Graham in any of the directories. Law enforcement officers shied away from making their personal information public for obvious reasons.

She tried a Google search and got a promising lead. A man named Custer Graham worked as a resource officer at a local high school. He appeared on Google as part of a newspaper article for instructing an in-service teacher education class on recognizing the signs of child abuse. Petronia knew school resource officer or SRO positions were often filled by retired members of law enforcement.

This could be her guy. Obviously, the school district wasn't going to give her his number either. She'd have to visit the high school and find him which presented her with a dilemma. Hobby cases were to be worked on her own time. School was in session during the day when she was supposed to be on duty. The high school was located outside her barracks patrol area.

Petronia contemplated asking Lieutenant Jardine for permission, but then she'd have to let him know why. Given the case was politically sensitive, he would order her to stand down, and she wasn't ready to do that yet. The old axiom played in her head: Better to ask forgiveness than to ask permission. Chances were she wouldn't be caught leaving the area. It would be a low risk move.

"You're going to get me into so much trouble, Barlow," she mumbled. His request had certainly set her on the path, but this was bigger than Barlow now. The case had gotten under her skin. An injustice was being perpetrated, and she wasn't going to let it stand.

18

CHAPTER 18

Barlow sat at a wobbly table at The Eight Ball with his boss, Irv Washington. He stuck a butter knife under one of the legs to keep it from shaking. The two men knocked off work early after completing construction on a section of town homes, getting them all under roof. They had caught up for the season and were almost out of work.

In between bites of his pork barbecue sandwich, Barlow filled Irv in on his trip to Pennsylvania and the opportunity to temporarily farm out workers to his late father's construction business.

Irv wore a big smile. "This is serendipity, son. I can hardly believe it."

Barlow set down his sandwich and wiped the corners of his mouth with a napkin. "If guys on our crew are willing to relocate to PA over the winter, there will be jobs for them. My father's construction business isn't officially mine until it clears probate, but once everything is squared away, we can form that partnership you keep bugging me about."

The big man clapped his hands together. "Outstanding!"

"I'm finding out I may have misjudged my old man." That thought made Barlow pick up his mug of beer and finish it off. He held it up for Caroline to see.

She sashayed over and took his mug. "How 'bout you, Irv, you need another?"

"Sure thing, doll." He passed his mug to her. "You don't mind me flirting with your girl, do you, Barlow?"

Caroline looked at Barlow and raised an eyebrow. When had it become commonly assumed that Caroline was now his girl? "I don't mind as long as she doesn't."

She winked at Irv. "You can call me doll anytime. Doesn't matter what Barlow has to say about it."

Irv winked back. "While you're at it, tune in the big screen to the Buckeye's replay on ESPN."

"You're such a football nut," she said while walking away.

They watched her. "That sweet, young thing is a great catch," Irv said. "You're a lucky man."

Yeah, lucky. Barlow wanted to change the subject. "I'll contact Les Cunningham, my father's foreman, to find out his specific needs and when he can be ready to take on our guys."

Caroline returned with their beers. "I need to get off my feet for a minute. Do you mind if I sit with you?"

Irv pushed out a chair with his foot. "We'd be delighted."

She sat between the two men.

Barlow pointed to his empty plate. "Tell them in the kitchen that my pork sandwich was delicious. Did you eat yet?"

"Too early. I'll grab a bite after happy hour." She faced Irv. "I couldn't help eavesdropping and heard Barlow explain about what's going on in Pennsylvania. Pretty cool, huh?"

"The timing couldn't be more perfect." Irv grew serious. "Uh, Barlow, Sorry man, I didn't mean that your father's death was timely."

Barlow waved him off. "Don't worry about it. I know what you meant."

"Anyway," Caroline continued. "I have a few days of vacation banked and will be riding along with Barlow during his next trip to PA. I've been to Pittsburgh a few times but never to the middle of the state."

"That so?" Irv asked with a big grin.

"You'll be bored," Barlow said. "Perry County is pretty to drive through, but there isn't much to do there."

"You'll find a way to keep me entertained." Caroline stood. "Gotta get back to work."

"I didn't realize things were at that stage between the two of you," Irv said. "Taking overnight trips together."

Barlow didn't respond. When Caroline first demanded to make the trip with him, he had an immediate negative reaction. Then he figured, why not? Having a pretty companion would make the long drive easier and the nights more pleasant. Given that he would need to spend time with Pet, Caroline would help divert his feelings from her and keep him centered. As an added bonus, Pet would see that he did indeed have a hot, young girlfriend, making him feel less of a loser around her.

She had moved on. Bringing Caroline with him and putting her on full display would prove to Pet that he had moved on too.

Uriah Collier stood at the window of his twentieth-floor penthouse office in center city Philadelphia admiring the view. He could see down the entire length of Broad Street to Pattison Avenue and the sports complex, even to the Walt Whitman bridge spanning the Delaware River into New Jersey.

He loved gazing out his windows in all four directions, counting the number of buildings he owned, or had once owned and sold. Counting his properties relaxed him. As one of the world's most successful real estate tycoons, Uriah enjoyed a lavish lifestyle and lacked for nothing. Although he considered Philadelphia his home, he owned getaway vacation mansions on Miami Beach, San Clemente Island in California, a mountain chalet in Estes Park, Colorado, a vineyard in South Africa, and a Spanish castle overlooking the Mediterranean.

During deer hunting season or when Uriah felt like slumming it, he escaped to his custom-built hunting lodge located on prime hunting grounds a few hours drive away in Perry County.

When he had been younger and building his empire, he had enjoyed spending time there. Pushing eighty and starting to feel his age, he wondered if it was time to sell the country lodge. He hadn't been there in many years.

The only thing stopping him was his only son, Howie Boy, who flew in from Idaho every year to hunt. Howie Boy would be arriving the week after Thanksgiving, his annual visit. The two of them, father and son, had agreed to review the succession plan for all of Uriah's businesses. Of course, he would pass everything on to his son, but that wouldn't happen soon. He had no plans of dying yet.

Uriah's personal assistant buzzed his desk phone. "Sir, you have two phone calls. The president is on line one."

He and the president of the United States enjoyed a respectful rivalry over the years, competing for the same building projects. Uriah had surpassed him a long time ago in terms of wealth. In terms of power? Well, being president was the pinnacle of power. He had to grudgingly admit the man had beaten him on those terms.

"Who's on the other line?" he asked.

"A police officer by the name of Tanzin."

Uriah froze. "Tanzin? He's calling me here?"

"Yes, sir."

The president could wait. "Send Tanzin's call through."

"Yes, sir."

The phone buzzed again and with a trembling hand he picked up the receiver. "Speak to me."

"Could be trouble." Sergeant Gus Tanzin was one of the many lackeys Uriah had on his payroll to monitor PSP activity.

"Go on."

"One of our female troopers called asking how to contact Detective Custer Graham. She told me it had to do with one of his unsolved cases."

Uriah sucked in a lung full of air. Detective Graham had retired with only one unsolved case. This couldn't be a coincidence. "I'll send a man to see you. Be prepared to brief him. Find out everything you can about this lady trooper."

"Got it. Any other action you want me to take?"

"No. Stay out of it. Maintain deniability. I'll handle things." He ended the call.

Uriah had received assurances that Detective Graham turned over all of the files concerning the incident from ten years ago. Now, for the first time since then, he worried some zealous cop might be prying into affairs that were none of her business.

If she found Custer Graham, would the former detective reveal any information? Uriah Collier second guessed himself. He should have had that man killed a long time ago.

19

CHAPTER 19

It wasn't unusual for a state trooper to meet with a school resource officer, so Petronia walked into the high school in her uniform but unannounced. She approached the front desk and asked for Custer Graham. The lobby was busy with teachers and students getting ready to start their day.

A few minutes later, a tall man approached wearing a navy-blue suit, white shirt with red necktie, and looking squared away. He appeared to be in his late fifties but still physically fit. Although he wasn't in a police uniform and didn't carry a firearm, she recognized him by his demeanor. Detective types never lost their swagger. Even after retirement they carried themselves in a certain way, cocky and confident.

"I'm Trooper Petronia Henning." She extended a hand.

The man had a firm grip, but not crushing. "I'm SRO Graham. What can I do for you?"

Straight to business. Petronia liked that. She hoped she wouldn't receive an urgent call, because she was outside her patrol area. The quicker she could get back the better. "Can we speak someplace private?"

Graham turned and motioned for her to follow. He led her into a conference room off the busy lobby area and closed the door. "Is this about a student? Is one of them in trouble?"

"I'm here to ask about your time with the PSP, specifically about one of your open unsolved cases, the convention center robbery."

Graham's eyes went wide. "I can't discuss that."

"Why not?"

"If you checked into it, then you know why."

She tried appealing to his ego. Men like him didn't like being reminded of their weaknesses. "Exactly who are you afraid of?"

He squinted. "Look, Trooper Henning, I was ordered to stand down and turn over my case files. I wasn't threatened. I have no reason to fear. I only followed orders." He looked at the clock on the wall. "Unless you have something else, we're done here. It's the start of a busy day."

He turned to leave. Petronia knew she had only one more shot. If she couldn't appeal to his ego, she might be more successful appealing to his sense of pride. "I understand you were one of the PSP's finest detectives. The convention center robbery was one of your only unsolveds. That has to bother you."

Graham laid his hand on the door knob but paused.

She kept talking. "I've only been a trooper for four years, but one thing I picked up on is how detectives always carry unsolved cases in the back of their minds. Even after they retire. Always thinking about them. Always puzzling out how there might be one string they could pull to make the case unravel and always looking for that string."

Graham remained silent.

"There's been a break in the case," she said. "Someone has come forward who may have knowledge about the missing money."

He turned to face her and pressed his back against the door. "Who else knows about this?"

"My barracks commander." A lie of omission, Petronia knew. Lieutenant Jardine had given her permission to work a hobby case, but he wasn't aware of the details. Graham didn't have to know that.

"Has the case been reopened?"

She had the urge to lie about that too, but her gut told her to play it straight. "No. If the connection to the missing money pans out we might be able to force the case back into the daylight."

Graham regarded her. "How exactly do you think I can help you?"

"Tell me what you know."

He took a few moments then pointed to the conference room table. "You better have a seat."

After they both sat, Graham spoke. "I don't have much to tell you. After the robbery, I interviewed the personnel at the convention center. All cash from paid parking and gate sales was secured in a high-tech vault on the premises. Their SOP was to leave the cash in the vault overnight and have it picked up by armored car early the next morning."

Petronia interrupted. "Did your case files include details of your interviews?"

Graham looked at her like she was incompetent. "Of course. Interviews, details of the armored car pickup, schedules, procedures, a detailed timeline, everything."

She knew an experienced detective would cover all the bases and felt a bit silly for having asked, but she wanted to verify that the case has been completely investigated. "A detailed timeline? When did the theft occur? When was it first reported?"

"The theft occurred after everyone left for the evening and the center was locked up."

She perked up. "How were you able to determine that?"

"Security camera. The robbery was well-thought out and professional. Alarm systems and central camera system were disabled, but there was one camera in the vault area independent of the main system. That camera time stamped the photos."

She gripped the side of the conference table. "Are you telling me you had photos? Face shots?"

"A little grainy but yes." He sighed. "As soon as the brass became aware of the photos, that's when I got shut down and was asked to turn over everything."

Petronia read something in his expression. "Did you turn over...everything?"

Graham hesitated. "Having to give up that case was the lowest point of my career with the PSP. The impropriety of it all kept me awake at nights until I eventually had to leave. Since I had enough years of service, I retired. Now I work for the municipal police as a SRO." He lowered his voice. "Shutting down that investigation was wrong. I still feel that way."

She pressed him. "You couldn't let go, could you? You still held onto something, maybe thinking one day you'd find that string to pull I mentioned earlier."

"You're treading into a mine field. If you keep pushing, very bad things might happen to you."

"That's my problem. What do you have?"

Graham looked her in the eye. "There were a lot of photos. I didn't think they would miss just one of them."

He had kept a photo of the perpetrator. She easily put it together. "Someone recognized the thief. Someone in power was trying to protect him or her. Who is the perp?"

Graham shrugged. "I honestly don't know. By the way, it's perps not perp. There were two of them."

20

CHAPTER 20

Barlow held the door for Caroline as they entered The Inn of the Dancing Bear. They had left Columbus before dawn on Tuesday morning after Thanksgiving and arrived just before lunch. The inn was deserted except for the old timer with the facial tick who sat at the far end of the bar. Barlow recalled his name, Twitchy. Caroline sauntered over to a bar stool while Twitchy gave her the once over.

The inn's owner popped out from the kitchen. Barlow waved him over but felt embarrassed because he had forgotten the man's name.

"You're back," the owner said. He looked at Barlow then at Caroline with a quizzical expression.

Barlow could read his mind. The guy was thinking, who is this lady? What happened to Pet? Of course, being a bartender, the man would never divulge the business of his customers. It was an unwritten code of conduct for bartenders everywhere. At least, that's what Barlow hoped.

"I'm Trevor Dunne," the bartender said as he extended a hand toward Caroline.

Caroline shook and introduced herself.

"Pleased to have you as a customer," Trevor said.

From his stool at the end of the bar, Twitchy slurred out the words, "Well now, she's a looker." He turned to Barlow. "This girl is classier than that woman cop you were with the last time."

Even though Barlow had told Caroline about his meetings with Pet, he felt his face grow hot with embarrassment. Why, though? He had nothing to feel guilty about.

Trevor snapped his fingers. "Hey, mind your own business, Twitchy. You leave these folks alone." He shook his head and wore an apologetic expression. "What can I get for you?"

Barlow glanced at Caroline. She acted as if Twitchy's unwelcome comment didn't faze her. To Trevor, she said, "We've been on the road for hours and haven't eaten. Is it possible to get a late breakfast?"

Trevor leaned against the bar. "Any other time of year your request would be no problem, but this is the second day of rifle season. In about fifteen minutes, this place is going to be teeming with deer hunters on lunch break from the woods who are going to be ravenous. My wife is busy in the kitchen preparing hot soups and chili getting ready for the rush."

"I feel what you're saying. For me it would be like during a Buckeyes game."

When the bartender cocked his head signaling he didn't understand what she was saying, Caroline went on. "I'm night manager at a busy sports bar in downtown Columbus, Ohio. When the Ohio State Buckeyes have a home game, it's complete chaos. We trim our menu back to serving just a few items to keep our kitchen staff from going bonkers, so I get it."

"I suppose you do."

She considered. "How about hot soup and a toasted cheese sandwich?"

"That I can do," Trevor said, "and out of professional courtesy to a fellow bartender, the meal is on me."

Caroline beamed. "Thank you."

"I'll have the same," Barlow said.

"Yeah, but you'll pay for yours." Trevor smiled. "Just kidding. How about drinks?"

"Water with lemon," Barlow said.

"Make that two," Caroline said.

From the end of the bar, Twitchy shouted, "Hey, I once spent an afternoon pulling drafts at the VFW. Do I get my meal for free?"

Trevor rolled his eyes and ignored the man.

"Before you fill our order," Barlow said, "there's another reason we're here. You told me during hunting season this place is booked solid, but we're going to need a room for a couple days. I've been gone too long from Perry County and lost touch with the businesses around here. Can you recommend someplace nearby?"

Trevor smiled. "You can stay here if you want. One of our reservations was a no show. I have an available room." He turned his attention to Caroline. "We have two guest bathrooms that you'd have to share with a horde of scruffy men deer hunters. Would that put you off?"

"Men I can handle." She gave Barlow a sidelong glance. "It's other women who cause me problems."

As soon as Petronia's shift ended, she drove into Harrisburg to the convention center for her meeting with the facility manager. When she had spoken with him over the phone, he hadn't seemed disturbed at all about being re-interviewed about the robbery. She waited for him in the lobby.

This was the final loose end she needed to clean up before her meeting with Barlow later that evening at the Dancing Bear. Thoughts of seeing him again made her belly flutter. Could she risk dredging up old feelings for him? Would that lead to her getting hurt again?

Petronia hated herself for not telling Barlow she was divorced, but she didn't want to appear like a loser in his eyes. It gave her a morbid kind of joy dressing up for him, making him realize what he had missed by ghosting on her. Or was she kidding herself? She was trying to encourage him. If he showed interest, she vowed to tell him about the divorce. Her swirling emotions were starting to give her a headache.

A short, portly man approached with his hand outstretched. "Trooper Henning, pleased to meet you. I'm Nate Grove."

She shook hands with the manager. His grip was limp, hand moist. "Thank you for agreeing to meet with me." She explained to him how she was working the cold case in her spare time.

Nate wore a serious expression. "I appreciate your effort. Anything you can find that might solve the case would be really helpful. The building, I can insure. Products, I can insure. But missing cash?" He shrugged. "I can't be insured for that. We took a huge loss."

He led her up the elevator into the security center. "This is where it happened." He pointed to a vault.

"How much cash was stolen?"

Grove raised an eyebrow. "Didn't you read the original detective's notes?"

If only she had access. "I'm just corroborating. I'd like to hear it again from you."

He shrugged. "A little over 223 thousand."

An amount that could feasibly be stuffed into a steamer trunk. She wondered what other information she could pry from this man.

The lady cop had been easy to follow. Lionel had lojacked her personal car and had been tracking her movements the past two days to find out for his employer, Uriah Collier, whether she really was following a trail from ten years ago and building a case .

The fact that she was here, talking with the convention center manager, told him all he needed to know.

He placed a call and reported the news.

From the other end of the line, his boss said, "You know what to do. Might as well deal with the retired detective too. We should've tied up that loose end long ago."

"Sir, you're sure? These are two law enforcement officers. Have you assessed the possible blowback from this action?"

"No, I'll just have to improvise if anything goes wrong." He sighed. "I'll do whatever it takes to protect Howie Boy."

21

Chapter 21

Petronia was pleased with herself, and she really hoped Barlow would be pleased with her too. The new information she had gathered might not lead to anything conclusive, but the details provided by Nate Grove and the contraband photo Detective Graham had given her made for some solid leads.

Feeling in a great mood, she decided to surprise Barlow by dressing up. The dress she chose was a respectable length but showed a lot of cleavage up top. Since it was cold, she slipped into a leather jacket.

She arrived early for their dinner meeting and didn't see Barlow anywhere in the restaurant or at the bar. She could've ordered a drink while waiting but decided instead to find him. Being a Tuesday night with no band, only a few customers sat at the bar and in the restaurant.

She got the attention of Anson, the night bartender, and asked which room Barlow was staying in.

"You're looking mighty fine tonight, trooper."

She secretly enjoyed when any man complimented her but usually never gave them the satisfaction of acknowledging. Instead, she gave him her most serious cop eye. "The room?"

He took his time admiring the view before answering her question. "Ten. Second to last room at the end of the upstairs hall."

Bursting with enthusiasm over wanting to share what she had found out during the investigation, Petronia didn't waste any time. She walked up the stairs, found room ten, and knocked.

The door opened. Instead of seeing Barlow on the other side of the threshold, a slender chick who appeared to be barely out of her teens greeted her, wearing a quizzical expression. "Can I help you?"

She scanned the small room. Nobody else there. She took a step back. "Sorry, I must have the wrong room number." Anson better have a good excuse for giving her the runaround.

The girl stood there, looking her up and down. Her eyes narrowed. "Are you the cop who is supposed to meet with Barlow?"

Confused, Petronia took a moment to process. Had Barlow picked up this chick at the bar? No. He wasn't the type to do that, and he certainly wouldn't tell a stranger about their meeting. As the wheels in her head spun, she considered how he wouldn't tell a stranger, but he would tell...a girlfriend. She raised a hand to her mouth. "Oh, god, no."

"You certainly don't dress like a cop." The girl's tone took on a sharp edge.

Self-conscious about the prominent cleavage displayed beneath her half-zipped leather jacket, heat crept into her face advertising her embarrassment. "I'm...I'm off duty." As she stuttered, she realized how lame her words sounded.

So, the bastard had the nerve to bring his girlfriend to their private rendezvous and not warn her about it ahead of time. She stood there feeling like an utter fool. Wanting to salvage some of her dignity, she extended a hand. "I'm Petronia."

"Yeah, he calls you Pet."

With her hand hanging in mid-air, Petronia couldn't recall ever having been so humiliated. Waves of hostility poured from the girlfriend. "Look, I don't know how much Barlow told you about me, but what happened between us has been over for a long time. We're friends now. Just friends."

The girlfriend leaned against the door frame, arms crossed at her chest. She said nothing. Although slight-built, the girl's demeanor advertised she would fiercely defend her claim on Barlow.

Petronia couldn't handle it anymore. "Tell Barlow I'll be down at the bar." She felt like pounding down a few shots.

When she turned to leave, the girl said, "Wait."

Petronia turned back.

The girlfriend nodded toward the room and sighed. "You might as well wait here."

Did this chick want to keep tabs on her, make sure she didn't accidentally bump into Barlow somewhere without her being there to chaperone? When the girl turned into the room, Petronia took the opportunity to zip up her leather jacket, all the way to her chin. She followed her in.

Girlfriend sat on the edge of the bed. Petronia took a seat in the room's only visitor chair. Feeling self-conscious, she pulled the hem of her dress, crossed her legs and tried to appear casual. "How about a do over? I already told you my name. What's yours?"

"Caroline." The girl paused. "You're a whole lot prettier than I expected."

"You're a whole lot younger than I expected."

The girl stiffened. "I'm not that young. I'm 22."

Six years younger than her and Barlow. Young. Gorgeous. Flawless complexion. A mane of hair to die for. Petronia felt utterly defeated. "Where is he?"

"Bathroom at the end of the hall. He wanted to shave." Caroline raised her eyes and met Petronia's gaze. "Now I know why."

"Did he tell you I was married?" Might as well keep up the ruse. The truth no longer mattered.

"You came here dressed like that, so does it really make a difference?"

Barlow walked into the room carrying his shaving kit and whistling a tune, completely oblivious to the tension between the two women. "Hello ladies, I see you've already met." He dropped his kit on the dresser and sat on the bed beside Caroline.

The room fell silent.

Barlow cleared his throat. "You look really nice tonight, Pet."

Caroline shot him a dirty look which he didn't see.

Petronia didn't know how to respond or if she should. She had been such an idiot getting her hopes up. Barlow had made it clear he was seeing someone, but she had mistakenly sensed that the relationship wasn't all that serious. He hadn't said much about Caroline during their previous encounters. She had completely misread him.

As the uncomfortable silence stretched on, Barlow looked at her and said, "You seem distant. Is anything wrong?"

Tears threatened to leak from the corners of her eyes, so she stood. "I'm hungry. Let's get something to eat."

From the smug, satisfied look on Caroline's face, Petronia knew it would be a long, unpleasant evening.

22

Chapter 22

A herd of boisterous men crowded around the bar, shouting over each other while sharing deer hunting stories. Pet followed behind Barlow and Caroline as he led them to a table far from the rowdies for some privacy. After they all sat, Barlow said, "It's busy tonight, and it may be a while until we get served. I'll order us a round of drinks. Beers everyone?"

Both women nodded and Barlow walked away.

The girl – that's how Pet continued to think of her – seemed to have chilled out. Where her expression had been pinched before, now she appeared more relaxed. She ran a hand through her thick mane, preening. "Barlow tells me the two of you have known each other like forever."

"We grew up together, but until last week I hadn't seen him in ten years."

"Has he changed much during that time?"

Pet had to be honest with herself. She had come tonight hoping for a chance to renew the romance she and Barlow once had. She realized now that had been a fantasy. "He's pretty much the same."

Pushing a strand of hair behind her ear, Caroline said, "Sometimes he seems distant, as if lost in thought. Has he always been so pensive?"

He had never been that way with her, always expressive, but they had been teens back then. The burden of thinking his father had been a murderer probably wore Barlow down. He had also served a tour with the Marines. Who knew what hell he had gone through there. "I don't think distant is the right word. Barlow could sometimes be mysterious though. In a good way. Like when he held things back in order to surprise me."

Barlow returned with their drinks. He set a beer in front of each of them. "Anson told me someone will be over in a few minutes to take our dinner order."

The girl got Barlow's attention. "Since you two were childhood buddies, what's the first thing you remember about Pet?"

She winced. When Barlow called her Pet, it was a term of endearment. This girl was being presumptuous thinking she could use her nickname. Also, what kind of a weird-ass question was that? What was she probing for?

"I suppose it was walking down the road together to go to the bus stop," Barlow said. He smiled and looked her way. "Remember? All the way back in first grade."

The thought warmed her. "You used to hold my hand."

His eyes lit up. "That didn't happen until a few years later."

"Oh no, you started holding my hand in first grade. In the spring. Trust me. A girl remembers these things."

Barlow turned in his seat, now fully focused on her. "Then second grade is when I must've started carrying your books."

"Wrong again. We didn't have homework in second grade."

"Maybe not, but we had show-and-tell. Remember?"

She snorted. "How could I forget that time with the hornet nest."

Barlow leaned toward her. "I climbed your dad's maple to cut it down during the winter. How was I supposed to know they were dormant inside that nest and would wake up when brought into a warm school building?"

She laughed. "The principal had to evacuate an entire wing of the school which did not go over well as I recall."

Barlow tapped the tabletop. "I'm not the only one to get into trouble with show-and-tell. How about the poison ivy incident?"

She groaned. "I thought you had forgotten."

"Are you kidding?" He chuckled and glanced over at Caroline. "We were studying poisonous plants that year, and Pet thought it would be cool to bring in a real live sample."

"Hey, I was careful. I recycled an old dill pickle jar and used garden gloves to take a cutting. I put the cutting in the jar and then screwed on the lid. Perfectly safe."

"Except you forgot to wash the outside of the jar where the plant made contact. You passed the jar around and everyone handled it. The next day, half the class was absent. The teacher got the worst of it."

Pet sighed. "We used to get into so much trouble together. Like the time we ditched school during the first week of trout season to go fishing."

Barlow snapped his fingers. "Yeah, we were in 7th or 8th grade. I called the school and pretended to be your dad to tell them you were sick, and you called the school pretending to be my mom."

"You didn't plan it quite well enough. We got caught because both calls were made from my parents' home phone. The principal got suspicious seeing the same caller ID."

Pointing at his chest, Barlow said, "Are you still blaming me for us getting caught?"

She couldn't hold back a smile. "Of course!"

Barlow studied her in a way that made her tingle inside. He said, "We both got detention, but it wasn't so bad, because we got to serve it together."

When the detention monitor wasn't looking, he had stolen a kiss from her. "I remember."

They went silent for a few beats. Barlow lowered his voice. "You and I were a pair, weren't we?"

Pet met his gaze. She couldn't hold back what she was thinking. "The happiest times in my life were when I was with you."

Things went quiet again as they held each other's gazes.

Caroline cleared her throat. For a few magic moments, Pet had completely forgotten about her. When she turned to face the girl, the expression on her face displayed a combination of boredom and annoyance. Too bad. She's the one who started them on the trip down memory lane.

"How much longer before someone comes to take our order?" the girl asked.

Scanning the room, Pet found Jill Dunne writing on a pad. The rowdies were apparently placing a complicated dinner order. A few moments later, she made her way over to them.

Just then, the bell above the door dinged and a couple with three kids entered followed by a big guy dressed in a pullover sweater and khakis. The family pushed two tables together and sat. The big guy sat alone at a nearby table.

The waitress tapped her pen against the order pad. "Sorry to keep you folks waiting."

"Hey, everyone, this is Jill," Barlow said. "She and her husband own this establishment."

Pet already knew that and said hello. The girl did likewise and introduced herself.

"What can I get you?" Jill asked.

"How about we split a pizza?" Pet suggested.

Barlow and Caroline also thought it was a good idea.

The bell above the door dinged as another couple entered.

Jill stomped her foot. "This is ridiculous."

The girl raised an eyebrow. "What? You're complaining? I would think you'd be happy that it's busy."

"I'm not complaining because it's busy. I'm upset that my waitress didn't show up for work. I have a call in to my husband to come and help us. He'll be here in twenty minutes, but in the meantime, Anson and I are running the place by ourselves."

Caroline pushed back her chair and stood. "Got an extra apron?"

Jill's eyes went wide. "You're a waitress?"

"A bar manager and a waitress. One of the best," Barlow told her.

"That's very generous of you," Jill said.

When Jill tried handing her the order pad, the girl waved her off. "Don't need one of those. I got this." She walked over to the big guy and asked him for his order.

A look of relief washed over Jill's face as she headed back to the kitchen. Pet felt relieved too, more relaxed, now that the girl was out of the way. She faced Barlow having pleasant thoughts of old times. She wanted to stay in that moment with him but didn't know how. Their moment had passed.

She sighed. "I have new information to share with you."

23

Chapter 23

A stab of melancholy shot through Barlow's core as he thought about his shared past with Pet. At the time, letting her go had seemed the right thing to do. Looking back, he now knew for sure it had been the biggest mistake of his life.

Nothing he could do about it now. She was married. What was her husband like? He hoped the man cherished her as much as he did. "I thought maybe you'd bring Charlie."

A facial tick crossed Pet's face as if she was troubled by the idea. "I didn't think tonight was going to be a social visit. We were supposed to be going over case details."

He could read her. Pet was upset he had brought Caroline. "I'm sorry. I didn't think you would mind Caroline tagging along."

She took a moment before responding. "It came as a surprise." She hesitated. "Barlow, don't you think maybe you're robbing the cradle? I mean, how much do you two really have in common?"

He didn't know how to answer.

Pet covered her mouth. "I'm sorry. It's really none of my business. The only important thing to me is that you're happy."

Barlow was satisfied with Caroline, but was he happy? He didn't like that disturbing thought and wanted to get off the topic. "What do you have to show me?"

Pet opened the small clutch she carried. She pulled two photos and passed them over.

Barlow studied them, holding them toward the light of the dim dining room. One photo showed a young man wearing a jacket and tie, like a school yearbook photo. The other photo showed two men, both angled toward the camera. Although grainy, he could still make out facial details. "What am I supposed to be seeing?"

"Do you notice any resemblance between the two photos?"

He looked closer. "Yeah. The yearbook photo is also one of the guys in the grainy photo."

"Do you recognize him?"

"No."

"It's Neil Mantener. Is that how you remember him when you pulled him from the car?"

"Not really. It could be him. It was dark. The guy was soaking wet, and I was scared. I can't remember that well; besides it was ten years ago."

She chuckled. "Relax, Barlow, this isn't an interrogation. I'm just asking."

Barlow felt a heavy hand come to rest on his shoulder. He turned and stared into the face of the big guy from the neighboring table.

The man removed his hand. "Excuse me. My first time here. Do you know where the bathrooms are?"

Pet pointed. "Over there on the other side of the bar. There's a short hallway."

"Thank you." The man walked away.

Barlow inspected the second photo, the one showing both men. "Where was this one taken?"

"Are you ready for this?" Pet paused for effect. "It's from a hidden camera in the security room of the convention center. It was taken hours before Neil Mantener's car crash. Those two men are the perpetrators."

Barlow could scarcely breathe. "That means—"

"—The cash you saw in the steamer trunk was real. You didn't imagine it."

He felt a great weight lift. Then another one dropped. "It proves nothing concerning whether or not my father stole the money or whether he did harm to Neil Mantener."

"Think about it, Barlow. There was an accomplice. Maybe you didn't see him. He could've taken the cash before your father got there."

"It was a big trunk. All that cash would've been heavy. How could the accomplice have gotten away without being seen? We both know our road has only one way in and out."

"I don't know. I don't have all the answers."

Barlow considered everything. "This is good work, Pet. How did you manage to put all this together? Why didn't law enforcement figure this out ten years ago?"

She detailed for him her meetings with former detective Custer Graham and Nate Grove, the convention center manager. "Without the cash linking the two cases, Neil Mantener's car crash looked like a random accident. There was no reason for anyone to suspect a connection."

It made sense. "Who is this second guy?"

"I don't know. I was hoping you might recognize him."

Barlow looked again. "As far as I know, I never met him. If he lived anywhere around our area, we would know him."

"Exactly my thoughts."

"Which means he's not a local."

"That would be my guess."

"You did great, Pet, I could kiss you."

His words had the desired effect. Her lips turned up into a smile. "I remember your kisses...and everything else that came after."

Barlow's heart rate accelerated. "I remember too. I'll never forget."

They held each other's gazes for a long moment. If the circumstances had been different...he needed to stop torturing himself. "So, where do we go from here?"

Pet leaned back in her chair, striking a sultry pose. "You mean your place or mine?"

He blushed, feeling flattered that she would still flirt with him. "What I meant was where do we go from here with the case?"

She grinned. "Did I just embarrass you?"

"Not at all."

"I think I did."

"Seriously, Pet, what's next?"

"We're at a dead end. Unless someone can recognize the second perpetrator, we know all there is to know."

"Show it all around. Put the photo in the newspapers. Get it on TV."

"Can't do that." She told him how the case was restricted and off-limits.

It angered him. "You mean someone is protecting this man?"

"I've already gone way out on a limb. I could lose my job." She leaned in. "But that doesn't mean you need to stop. Keep the photo. Show it around. If you get a hit, let me know."

He slipped the photo into his shirt pocket. When he looked at Pet, an empty feeling filled him. "I guess this is it."

She cocked her head. "What?"

Barlow swallowed. His throat felt dry. "This case was the reason for us to see each other again. I don't know when we'll get another opportunity."

Pet rested her arm on the table. "I'm happy we got this chance. You made me recall sweet memories, but Barlow, we can't easily undo what's been done. Our lives have changed. You're with Caroline now, and I'm...I'm—"

"—I know, you're married." This woman who completed him so fully was now out of reach. They could never be lovers again, and the ache in his chest made it clear it would be too painful for them to even remain friends.

24

Chapter 24

Petronia had paced herself during her meeting with Barlow and his girlfriend, limiting herself to two beers. The last thing she had wanted was to lose control of her inhibitions and make an even bigger fool of herself than she already had. She drank one beer before pizza and one afterward.

As she drove herself home, she thought of the memories dredged up of her past with Barlow. Those thoughts filled her with melancholy. It was truly over now, she knew, with no possibility of resurrecting what they once had. Barlow seemed happy with Caroline and there was no reason for the two of them to ever see each other again. She had done all she could for Barlow and had given him the photograph. It was up to him if he wanted to show it around.

She fully intended to come clean with him tonight about her divorce. It bothered her how she had lied to him. But now? She hadn't been able to tell him with Caroline being present.

What did it matter anyway now that she knew for sure Barlow and Caroline were a couple?

In the dark, a pair of headlights came up on Petronia fast and rode her bumper. High beams reflected from her rear view mirror and blinded her. She slowed and eased her car close to the berm in order to allow the car to pass. Whoever was behind her didn't get the message. She slowed even more and powered down her side window. She stuck out an arm and waved the driver forward.

The driver just hung there behind her.

Why didn't this idiot pass her? A curve in the road loomed ahead of them with a no passing zone.

She sighed and wished she were in uniform. She would give this driver a piece of her mind about following too closely and with high beams. As she neared the curve, her car lurched.

She gasped. "I think that asshole just rear ended me." Her car accelerated.

With a sickening feeling, Petronia realized she was being pushed. "What the hell?" She jammed on her brakes, but that caused her to lose control as the vehicle pushing her continued to accelerate.

She would never make it around the curve. Her car crossed the center line and went airborne as it left the road and nosed down an embankment.

An airbag exploding in her face was the last thing she remembered before passing out.

Lionel pulled to the side of the road, switched off his headlights, and powered off the motor. He looked both ways. Nobody coming. The sparsely traveled rural road had been the perfect spot for an ambush, especially at night.

The lady cop's compact car had been no match for the Dodge Ram pickup he had stolen from a Harrisburg construction site. Pushing her from the road had been as easy as sweeping aside a dust mote from a tabletop. Now, all he needed to do was finish the job.

Pulling a tactical flashlight from his inside jacket pocket, Lionel got out of the car and made his way across the lane. He stepped down the bank into the meadow below.

When the car left the road, it had sideswiped a utility pole, spun in midair, smashed grill first into the ground, and rolled onto its roof. The impact probably killed her, making his job easier. Uriah Collier wanted her dead, so he needed to make sure, but he also needed to make it look like an accident.

Lionel shone his flashlight all around to verify she hadn't been ejected from the car. He approached the driver side. The door had sprung open when the car buckled. He bent down to take a look inside.

His target hung from her seat belt, upside down in her seat, unconscious, face resting against the deployed airbag. He placed two fingers against the side of her neck, felt a pulse. Still alive.

She didn't appear to be bleeding anywhere seriously enough, but her nose was bent to the side, broken, thanks to the airbag impact.

What a shame. The lady cop had looked gorgeous in her dress. A pang of regret filled him as he realized how much this woman reminded him of his own daughter. She was around the same age and build.

How had it come to this, becoming his boss's hit man? Twenty years ago, he had signed on with Uriah Collier as personal security. That job evolved from one of protecting his boss to becoming his henchman. At the time, he needed the generous salary offered to perform dirty deeds. He had rationalized with his conscience. His wife had been sick, insurance wouldn't cover the experimental treatment she needed, and they had a little girl who depended on him.

Lionel eased Petronia's head into the crook of his elbow and placed his other hand on her shoulder. One quick twist would do the job, the torque snapping her neck. It wouldn't be questioned. It would appear as if she had broken her neck in the car crash.

He hesitated, thinking again how this could be his daughter.

From the road above, tires crunching gravel on the berm of the road interrupted him. Someone was pulling to a stop. He cursed, backed away from the wrecked car, and stood.

The beam of a flashlight pieced the darkness and found his face. Lionel raised a hand to shield his eyes. "Who are you?"

"Police," a harsh voice answered. "What happened here?"

Of all the times for a cop to be driving by. Lionel knew he wouldn't be able to finish the job now. He needed to get away. "There's been an accident. I was behind this car and saw it drive off the road. I stopped to see if I could help."

The cop shone his flashlight at the crashed car. "How many occupants?"

"One as far as I can tell. A lady. She's still breathing but appears to be in a bad way."

"Step aside," the cop uttered. He climbed down the embankment.

"While you check on her, I'll get a blanket from my vehicle. We should keep her warm until an ambulance arrives."

"Thank you," the cop said.

They passed each other on the bank. Lionel wasted no time. He climbed into his stolen truck and drove off.

Half-an-hour later, he merged into traffic on the interstate feeling confident he had successfully eluded any possible pursuing troopers. The cop at the scene hadn't gotten a good look at him in the darkness and hadn't had time to run his license plate. He returned the stolen truck to the construction site and climbed into his own vehicle.

While driving away, Lionel touched the speed dial button for his employer.

Uriah Collier picked up on the third ring. "Speak to me."

"The job's done," Lionel lied.

"Tell me the details."

Was the man crazy? "Boss, let me remind you we are on unsecured cell phones."

Collier's voice came back sharp. "That's my concern. Tell me what happened."

The old man was losing it. He mistakenly thought he was invincible, that nobody could touch him. When it came to protecting his son, the man had become reckless. "The woman met with an accident. A fatal car crash."

"Fatal you say?"

"Affirmative."

"And the former detective?"

Custer Graham was a loose end from ten years ago, a loose end Uriah now wanted cleaned up. "Double tap." Lionel didn't need to elaborate. The old man knew it meant one shot to the chest and one to the head. "Apparently, the man got in the middle of a drug deal between two of his students who fled the scene." At least, that's the way Lionel staged it. Pills strewn about. A bundle of cash.

"Excellent!" Uriah said. "Howie Boy should finally be in the clear with no more worries." He terminated the call before Lionel could say anything else.

There was a lot more he should say. The situation had cascaded out of control.

He didn't know how the lady cop had obtained the photo of Howie Boy with Neil Mantener, but she was clearly on to something. The young man now knew. So did his girlfriend. So did all the patrons in the bar when the young guy starting showing the photo around. He couldn't kill them all. Luckily, nobody recognized Howie Boy from the photo. Not yet. It was only a matter of time.

Lionel sighed. Time to rid himself of this job. He had amassed enough of a nest egg to flee to a haven he had been researching in Costa Rica. His wife was now many years gone, having eventually succumbed to the terrible illness that had eaten away at her. His daughter was married with her own family, living far away from the likes of Uriah Collier.

With his bug out bag resting on the back seat, Lionel pointed his car in the direction of Harrisburg International Airport. Tomorrow, he would be living a new life.

As for Howie Boy? Lionel couldn't help grinning. From what he had witnessed tonight, the determination in that young man's expression while showing the photo around, Howie Boy's problems were just beginning.

25

Chapter 25

Nobody Barlow showed the photo to could identify the mystery man. Feeling discouraged, he wondered if he should just drop the whole thing. Except something inside wouldn't allow him to do that. He had to know. All these years he had blamed his father for killing Neil Mantener and stealing the cash.

Those thoughts plagued him as he drove to his meeting with Les Cunningham and his crew. Caroline sat in the passenger seat, gazing out the side window, brooding. Since their meeting with Pet last night, she had been acting moody.

He understood. She felt threatened by his history with Pet and their ease and familiarity with each other. Barlow reached across the console and took her hand. She let him, but he could tell her heart wasn't in it. He figured once they returned to Ohio and Caroline was back on her home turf, she'd snap out of her funk.

He eased his van onto the gravel lot of his father's construction office, his construction office now. That concept was still hard to get used to. His former boss, Irv Washington, now his partner--another hard concept to get used to--had already arrived. His pickup sat in the lot near the door. They had arranged an orientation meeting with his father's crew to bring everyone up to speed on the merger. Irv had arrived late last night but opted to stay in more comfortable accommodations in one of the chain hotels at the Carlisle turnpike exit.

He and Caroline walked across the gravel lot and entered the modular office.

A half-dozen sets of men's eyes inspected them as they entered. They gave Barlow a quick glance before settling on Caroline.

"Les already introduced me to the crew," Irv said.

"What's left of the crew," Les added. "Sam, Tom, Frank, and Allen are the only ones remaining."

The four employees shook hands with Barlow.

"This is my girlfriend, Caroline," Barlow put an arm around her waist.

"Pleased to meet you, Caroline," Les said. "Would you and Barlow like coffee?"

Barlow waved him off. "No thanks, I had plenty of coffee at the inn this morning."

Caroline eyed the Keurig machine. "I'll have coffee, but I'll get it myself. You men have things to discuss."

They all watched her as she selected a K-cup and popped it into the hopper.

Barlow cleared his throat. When they refocused on him, he said, "Thank you all for sticking with the company. I came here to assure you that everything is going to proceed as usual. You will continue to get paid. Les Cunningham has been your foreman under my father, and he will continue in that role along with taking on some additional responsibilities." He went on to explain how a contingent of workers from Ohio would fill in over the winter until new local labor could be hired in the spring.

After a short Q & A session, everyone seemed satisfied.

Les grabbed his car keys from the desk. "Barlow, Caroline, and Irv are going to follow us to our housing project in New Bloomfield where I'll give them a tour. The rest of you guys can get to work. You all know what to do."

As the men started shuffling toward the door, Barlow suddenly remembered. "Oh, wait." He reached into his jacket pocket and pulled out the photo. "Do any of you recognize these guys?"

The men passed it around, all of them shaking their heads. They headed out. Barlow heard them start their vehicles and drive off.

Les Cunningham gave the photo a good look and also shook his head. "What's this about?"

Barlow took the photo back from him. "Never mind."

"Let me see," Irv said and extended his hand to take it.

Living his entire life hundreds of miles away in Columbus, the chances of Irv knowing who the mystery man was seemed slim to none. Barlow didn't see the point but passed the photo to Irv anyway so he wouldn't feel left out.

Irv studied the photo for a few seconds and smiled. "Yeah, I know him."

Barlow felt something like an electrical charge surge through him. "What? Are you sure?"

Caroline sucked in a sharp intake of air and moved to Barlow's side.

"Of course. It's—"

Before he could finish, the office door burst open with such a force, it bounced against the door stop. A disheveled man wearing a dirty wool shirt stumbled in holding a pint bottle of spirits. He raised a shaking finger and pointed it at Barlow. "Are you Forrest's kid?"

Les came around from behind the desk and approached the man. "What are you doing here?"

"Answer me!" the man shouted. Caroline flinched and took a step back.

"I'm Barlow Jackson. Forrest was my father. Who are you and what do you want?"

The man wobbled on his feet. "So, you're the sum o' bitch who fired me."

Les spoke up. "This is Slay Gunther, the former employee I told you about. The one who got into trouble with a state trooper while driving one of our vehicles."

Barlow recalled giving Les permission to fire the man. "Yeah, I'm responsible for canning your ass, and seeing the condition you're in, I'm surprised my father ever hired you in the first place."

Les pointed at the door. "Slay, you have ten seconds to get the hell out of here before I call the police. Don't ever come back."

The drunkard cackled. "At least it won't be that crazy woman who arrested me the last time."

This man was arrested by a lady trooper? Barlow took that to be too much of a coincidence. He had to be referring to Pet.

"Your time is up." Irv pulled his cell phone.

"Bitch got what she deserved. She won't be arresting anybody ever again."

Barlow reached over and closed his hand around Les's, stopping him from making the call. "Wait a minute." He turned to the drunkard. "Who are you talking about?"

"I got this, Barlow." Les moved toward the man. Barlow figured he was going to bodily remove the guy from the office.

"Wait!" Barlow shouted.

Everyone froze. The drunkard wore a smirk.

"Who are you talking about?" Barlow asked. "What do you mean she got what she deserved?"

The drunkard made a grand sweeping gesture with his arm. "The one with the Italian sounding name."

Caroline gasped and put a hand over her mouth. She uttered, "Petronia."

The drunkard rocked on his feet. "Yeah, that's the one. She got what she deserved."

When Barlow was with the Marines, he heard men speaking about blood lust, the uncontrollable desire to kill while in the heat of battle. It's something he had never experienced...until that moment.

He lunged, grabbed the man by the collar of his coat, and slammed him against the wall. The pint bottle the man held went flying across the room. Barlow slammed the man again, the back of his head bouncing off the wall, his eyes going wide and panicky.

"What have you done?" Barlow shouted. "What did you do to Petronia?"

From behind him, he heard an amused Irv Washington say, "You go, Barlow!"

The man's hands came up and scrabbled against Barlow's arms. "Let go of me, man. I have a torn rotator cuff."

Barlow slammed the back of the man's head against the wall, harder. "If you harmed her, I'll break every bone in your body."

The man's eyes seemed to roll up into his head.

Caroline wedged herself between Barlow and the drunkard. "Stop it, stop it," she urged. "Barlow, you're killing him."

A moment later, the three of them, Caroline, Irv, and Les pried Barlow off of the man.

Slay Gunther slid against the wall to the floor and came to rest on his butt, legs splayed in front of him. Drool leaked from a corner of his mouth.

Les knelt to get eye level with the man. He spoke in a calm tone. "Slay, what are you trying to tell us about the lady trooper? Did you do anything to her?"

He gave Barlow a suspicious look before turning his gaze back to Les. "Not me, man. I didn't do nothin'. Bitch had an accident. Saw it on ABC 27 news this morning."

26

Chapter 26

When Barlow and Caroline arrived at the hospital, they had to wait in line outside Pet's room. In front of them were two uniformed state police troopers who eyed the two of them.

Barlow introduced himself and Caroline. "Petronia and I grew up together. We're good friends."

The troopers identified themselves and shook hands. They were Lieutenant Martin Jardine and Trooper Morg Johansson. Both men wore squared away uniforms, crisp ironed trousers, perfectly knotted ties, and highly polished shoes. Jardine said, "We work with Petronia and respect the hell out of her. She's an ace trooper."

Since the man was a lieutenant, Barlow figured he was her boss. "Can you tell me what happened? The news report lacked details."

"It's one of the reasons we're here," Jardine said. "We need to talk with her about the accident."

"I hope she's okay," Caroline interjected.

Trooper Johansson fingered the brim of his hat. "We spoke with her doctor a few minutes ago. She's banged up pretty bad but nothing life threatening."

Barlow sighed in relief. The knot in his stomach eased.

The room door opened and a nurse and Pet's mother exited. She nodded to the two troopers. "She's ready to talk with you now."

The lieutenant snapped to attention. "Thank you, ma'am." He turned to Barlow. "It will be a while until we're done interviewing her. You might want to get coffee."

He acknowledged the lieutenant with a nod. "Mrs. Henning, do you remember me?"

She regarded him. "Barlow Jackson. What a pleasant surprise. It's been years."

"Ten to be exact." He embraced Pet's mother. When they separated, he introduced Caroline.

"How is Petronia?" Caroline asked.

"Broken nose, stitches in her forehead that will leave a nasty scar, black eyes, swollen face, but the doctors assured us there are no internal injuries. Thank God for seat belts and airbags."

"Were any other vehicles involved?"

Mrs. Henning shook her head. "It appears to be a one car accident. She simply ran off the road."

Barlow knew Pet only had two beers and they were spaced an hour apart. She couldn't have been seriously impaired. She patrolled the county roads, knew them well. How could she have missed a turn?

"We were with Pet before it happened." Barlow went on to explain to Pet's mom how the three of them had dinner together at the Dancing Bear but left out details concerning the purpose of their meeting.

"Petronia didn't tell me you were back. Where do you live?"

Barlow explained how he lived in Ohio and how his father's passing led to a chance encounter with Pet.

"I knew your father had passed because of us being neighbors. Sorry for your loss."

"Thanks."

"I occasionally get phone calls from your mother. How is she doing?"

"Fine. I was hoping to fly to Texas to visit with her over the holidays."

Mrs. Henning checked her watch. "I'm so happy to have seen you again. Stop by and see me sometime. You spent so much time at our house growing up that I was practically your second mother. When you see your mother, please send her my regards."

"I certainly will."

She turned to walk away, Barlow thought about something. "Wait, Mrs. Henning?"

When the woman stopped, Barlow asked, "Where's Petronia's husband, Charlie? I thought he would be here."

An odd expression crossed Pet's mother's face. She cocked her head. "Charlie? Goodness, Barlow, Charlie is remarried and lives in Maryland. He hasn't been in the picture for a long time."

Petronia wished she could be more helpful to her lieutenant about the accident. Her head hurt, and details about the previous night were fuzzy. The last thing she remembered was driving home after meeting with Barlow and Caroline. She had no idea how she had crashed her car. She couldn't remember how many beers she had. The doctor told her memory loss was typical following a trauma. He also said in time she'd probably recover her memory.

"How poorly will this reflect on me?" she asked Lieutenant Jardine. "Am I going to lose my job?"

"I'll be honest with you. That depends on the tox screen."

She had voluntarily submitted to his request for a blood sample figuring it would look bad if she refused him. It worried her, though, because she couldn't remember. Had she been impaired?

"The roads were dry," Morg said, the implication being she had no excuse for leaving the road. "The berm is plenty steep at that spot. If I hadn't come upon the car stopped at the side of the road, I hate to think how long it might've been 'till someone found you."

Petronia tried making sense of his words. "Someone stopped?"

"A man said he saw it happen. He came to your assistance."

She had a vague notion of having been followed. "Who?"

Morg shrugged. "I didn't have the opportunity to ID him, because my priority was to tend to you. He left shortly after I got there. I guess he figured I'd handle it."

"Thank you, Morg, for being there for me."

The trooper seemed embarrassed. He looked at the floor. "No problem, Petronia. You'd do the same for me."

Lieutenant Jardine laid a hand on her shoulder. "If you remember anything else about what happened, call me. Don't worry about your job. Worry about getting better."

The two men left and a heavy weariness settled on her. She hurt. She wanted to sleep.

"Pet?"

A familiar voice. She opened her eyes. Barlow. The look of pity on his face made her feel wretched. "Go away. I don't want you to see me like this."

Instead of leaving, he took her hand. "You said those exact words during our sophomore year of high school, remember?"

She closed her eyes. "No. What are you talking about?"

Barlow chuckled. "You had a huge zit on the tip of your nose. We were supposed to go to the homecoming dance, but you refused to go."

Now she remembered. "We compromised. You agreed we didn't have to go to the dance since I was too embarrassed, and I agreed you could spend the evening with me anyway, despite my zit."

"It was one of the most fun dates we had."

She kept her eyes closed and allowed the memory to replay. "We had our own private party. A picnic on my parent's front porch. We sat on the porch swing."

"I serenaded you with your dad's guitar."

Petronia giggled. "You were terrible, Barlow. Couldn't carry a tune if your life depended on it."

He squeezed her hand. "But I made you forget you had a zit."

His words were true. "You were so good to me."

"You had an iPod back then," Barlow said. "We danced, remember?"

She opened her eyes. "We shared a set of earphones. I wore the right side and you the left. The only way that worked was when you held me close and we slow danced."

"I'll never forget that night," he said.

Petronia heard the slats of the window blinds rattle. Was someone else in the room? She turned her head and saw Caroline. Pulling her hand from Barlow's, she said, "Oh, hello, I'm sorry. I didn't see you there. I didn't mean to ignore you."

The girl approached and did the strangest thing. She flashed a rueful smile and ever so gently placed a hand against her cheek. She held it there for a long moment before saying, "You take care of yourself, Petronia. I'm going to get some air and make a phone call."

"I won't be much longer," Barlow said to Caroline as she headed for the door.

Without another word, the girl left them alone. As soon as she left, Barlow sighed. "Pet, I had a conversation with your mother."

"That's nice. I'm sure she was glad to see you again after all this time."

"She was, and it was nice seeing her again too."

Something about the way he was looking at her. Her mother. And... "Oh god, oh no."

"Why didn't you tell me the truth about your divorce?"

Tears leaked from her eyes. She cursed. "I'm crying. I haven't cried since our breakup. Not even when my father passed away. Damn it all, Barlow, now my humiliation is complete. You always put me on such a high pedestal. You left because you didn't think you were good enough for me. Look what happened. I'm a failure as an adult, couldn't even hold onto a marriage, and now I'm disfigured."

She rolled to her side and sobbed, faced the window, unable to look at Barlow's face any longer. "Leave me alone. Caroline is waiting for you."

Barlow stroked her hair. "Don't be silly. You are not disfigured, Pet. Your face is going to heal good as new." He leaned close and whispered in her ear. "Even if it didn't, you will always be beautiful to me."

27

CHAPTER 27

The plan had been for Barlow, Caroline, and Irv to return to Columbus after touring the New Bloomfield construction site. Things had gone awry as a result of Pet's accident and they started late. By the time they finished the tour, it was nearly dinner time.

Caroline wasn't brooding anymore. In fact, it seemed as if a strange calm had settled over her.

Instead of driving directly back to Columbus after the inspection tour, they decided to grab a bite to eat at The Dancing Bear before hitting the road together. Depending on traffic, the drive home could take seven or eight hours, so they weren't going to arrive until well after midnight.

They decided to sit at the bar instead of a table. The place was moderately busy, but Anson, the night bartender, waited on them right away. Irv ordered a beer and club sandwich, Caroline wanted a water and taco salad.

"I'll have a burger and a black coffee," Barlow said. "Long drive tonight. I'll need to stay awake." That made him think of Pet's accident. He couldn't imagine how she messed up so badly.

Jill Dunne popped into the bar from the kitchen carrying a stack of beer mugs fresh from the dishwasher. Steam from the mugs trailed in her wake. She saw Caroline and approached, set the rack of mugs on top of the bar. "Thanks again for helping out last night. You made a big difference."

"No problem. It was fun."

"Are you sure I can't pay you for your time?"

Caroline waved her off. "You let me keep my tips. That's payment enough."

Jill picked up the rack. "If you ever want a job, come and see me."

"Thank you. I'm flattered. Don't take this the wrong way. It's beautiful country around here, but I'm a city girl. I'm more comfortable in Columbus."

Jill walked to the other end of the bar and started putting mugs back on the shelf. "If you ever change your mind..."

"It really is pretty around here," Irv said, "the trees and mountains, but I'm afraid I'd soon get bored. How are we going to do this, Barlow? Are you thinking about relocating back to PA to be closer to your half of the business?"

He was torn. Les Cunningham could certainly manage his father's business without him. The man was capable enough. Barlow would have to put in an appearance once a week or so. He could handle that. He also admitted to himself how much he missed Perry County, and he could occasionally drop in on Pet.

"I don't know, Irv. Let's take it a step at a time and see how it plays out."

"Fair enough."

Anson returned with their drinks. He set a steaming cup of coffee in front of Barlow. Too hot to drink right away.

Barlow remembered the unfinished business he had with Irv. After Petronia's accident, identifying the man in the photo had seemed less important. Now was a good time to bring up the subject again. He pulled the photo from his pocket and slid it down the bar to the big man.

Irv picked it up. "Yeah. It's him."

"Who?" Caroline asked. Her wide eyes displayed genuine curiosity.

"Howard Collier. They call him Howie Boy."

Barlow and Caroline both sat there looking at Irv. Caroline broke the silence. "Is that supposed to mean something to us?"

Irv chuckled. "Probably not. You would have to be a college football nut like me to remember this guy. He played defensive end for Penn State about ten years ago. I remember how he ruined the Buckeye's season by intercepting a fourth quarter pass. Cost them the game and their number one ranking."

Barlow turned that information over in his mind but could make no sense of it. He remembered from the obituary how

Neil Mantener had been a Penn State student. Is that where he and this Howie Boy character met?

He took a sip of coffee. Still too hot to drink. "Whatever happened to him?"

Irv shrugged. "Once these guys leave college, I can't keep track of them. He never went pro as far as I know."

Howie Boy Collier. Barlow now had a name. If he could find this man, he might finally get to the truth. He'd have to proceed with caution though. The man had committed a crime by robbing the convention center, and maybe he had something to do with the death of Neil Mantener.

"What's it all about?" Irv asked.

Barlow didn't want to get into it and was saved from doing so when their food arrived. "I'll tell you later."

By the time they finished eating, it was fully dark outside. The cup of coffee had been a good idea. A long drive at night was never Barlow's idea of fun. "You ready to hit the road?"

Irv and Caroline both agreed. Barlow paid their bill.

"You going to wait for us while we pack?" Barlow asked Irv. "We can caravan together."

Irv and Caroline exchanged glances. "Yeah, I'll come up to the room with you and wait."

As they climbed the staircase, Barlow halted and took another look at the bar and restaurant below. Nice place. He'd be back. Maybe over the weekend, to visit Pet. He promised he'd visit, and after witnessing how depressed she was, he was plenty worried about her.

There really wasn't much to pack. He and Caroline had been living out of overnight bags. Barlow took one last look around. "Well, that's it."

Standing by the door, Irv asked, "Are you ready, Caroline?"

"Be right with you. Can you give us a minute?"

Irv nodded and left the room.

Caroline picked up her bag. "Barlow, I'm riding back to Columbus with Irv."

"What? Why?"

"Because you need to stay."

His head spun as he tried to decipher what she was trying to tell him.

She approached and kissed him on the cheek. "I know you care about me, but you will never love me the way you love her."

"Caroline, I'm with you."

She shook her head. "You don't mean that. Not really. You're just being gracious and don't want to hurt me. It's okay, Barlow. Your place is with her. The love you two have for each other." She stopped. Barlow thought she might cry, but she took a breath. "It's beautiful, the history the two of you share, in love with each other since childhood. It may sound corny, but you were made for each other. It's so plain to see."

"Look, Caroline—"

"—Don't argue with me. God, Barlow, you nearly killed a man over her. I hope someday I'll find someone who will love me that much. Stay. Go to her. You need each other. Be happy."

He didn't know what to say.

Caroline went to the door. "I'll see you back at The Eight Ball."

And then, she was gone.

28

Chapter 28

Ten Years Ago (Part 1)

Howie Boy Collier walked across campus feeling dejected. The rainy August evening added to his funk. After football practice today, he had spoken with a pro scout who told him he wasn't quite big enough, strong enough, or fast enough to make it as an NFL defensive back.

He couldn't understand it. He was about to enter his senior year at Penn State University and the coach had named him as a starter on defense. How could he be playing for one of the most elite college football teams in the country and not even be considered for the draft?

He had some serious sulking to do. A few minutes later he found himself sitting in a bar in downtown State College, PA. It wasn't one of the more popular places, so it wasn't busy. A few people sat in booths and a foursome played pool in the game room.

"Bourbon, straight up," he told the bartender, "and a beer chaser." His father had introduced him to the joys of bourbon when he had turned twenty-one. He didn't like the stuff much but couldn't argue with how quickly it worked to remedy his sour moods. When the bartender set the spirits and mug of beer in front of him, Howie Boy threw back the bourbon savoring the burn to his throat and chest. He put out the fire with a long pull of cold beer.

"Another," he ordered. The bartender was only too happy to oblige. Howie Boy had the reputation of being a big tipper when the wait staff showed him special attention.

From a booth behind him, a voice asked, "Woman troubles?"

Howie Boy swiveled on the bar stool and recognized Neil "Manty" Mantener, a student who had been on the same floor of his freshman and sophomore dorm. Although they both took some of the same classes, they didn't have the same circle of friends, Howie Boy being an avowed jock and Neil Mantener a nerdy electrical engineering major. At keggers, though, the nerd loosened up and was always good for a few laughs.

"What makes you think I have woman troubles?"

Manty sat in a booth, books piled high, stacks of papers strewn about, a plate of nachos sitting near his left elbow, and holding a mug of beer in his right hand. "Looks like you're planning to go on a bender. Most of the time that behavior can be traced back to problems with a woman."

The bartender delivered Howie Boy's second round. He picked up his drinks and joined Manty in his booth. "For your information, Sherlock, you're way off base in your deduction. It isn't about a woman." He eyed the nachos.

Manty noticed him looking and slid the plate of nachos his way. Howie Boy grabbed a few of the chips and laid them on a paper napkin.

"What then?" Manty asked. "Why the long face?"

Howie Boy downed his second bourbon and snapped his fingers, signaling the bartender for a third.

"I wish I had the power to do that, have people come running when I snapped my fingers."

"Has nothing to do with power. It's all about how much money a person is willing to spend."

"Ah, but money equals power."

With his head already gone fuzzy, Howie Boy considered his classmate's statement. "Yeah, money. It's a double-edged sword. When you have too much money people become jealous of you." He had a sudden revelation. That had to be it! "Those sons-of-bitches are jealous of my father's success and wealth. This is their way of getting back at him. Through me. That's why I'm being black-balled. All the team owners are conspiring against him and me. They're telling the scouts to ignore me."

Manty set down the paper he had been reading. "What are you mumbling about?"

It was crystal clear to Howie Boy. Someday, he'd be in a position of power to get back at those old bastards, the cartel of NFL owners. He might run for congress, maybe even president, and tax the hell out of them. Make them sorry for what they're doing to him.

Manty tapped the tabletop with his finger. "You okay, bro?"

"Yeah, yeah, I'm fine. Never mind."

The bartender delivered his third round.

"Set Manty up with another round, on me," he told the man, "and bring another plate of nachos."

When the bartender walked away, Howie Boy viewed all the junk Manty had piled on the table. "What's all this? Classes don't start for another two weeks. It can't be an assignment."

"Getting an early start on a case study we're going to have this semester in engineering class. I need to keep up my GPA to have an edge when applying for jobs in the spring."

Howie Boy never had to worry about his GPA. He had a guaranteed job waiting with one of his father's companies as soon as he earned his degree. The stack of materials had him curious though. "What are you researching?"

"A major manufacturer of bank vault locking mechanisms is experiencing a malfunction in one of their popular models. Sometimes the locks won't release after the correct code is entered."

Howie Boy chuckled. "I can understand how that can lead to dissatisfied customers."

"When it happens, it can cause quite a panic. The company found a problem with the software and released a patch. Technicians can provide a temporary fix by uploading new code into the lock's firmware."

"I could never be a coder. Too boring."

"You wouldn't say that if you came across what I did during my research."

"Oh, yeah? Like what?"

Manty went quiet for a moment. He sat back in his seat. "Forget it."

"Oh, no," Howie Boy waved a finger in front of Manty's face. "You can't take back what you said. Why are you all excited about this?"

Manty closed his eyes and squeezed the bridge of his nose with his fingers. When he opened his eyes he looked all around, bent closer, and lowered his voice. "Look, you can't tell anyone what I'm about to tell you."

Yeah, the nerd was good for laughs. He'd play along. With the buzz Howie Boy had going, chances were, he'd forget all about it tomorrow morning anyway. "C'mon, Manty, you and I are amigos from the same dorm. You can tell me."

Manty's voice went even lower. "The company provided their original source code to the university as part of the electrical engineering case study. I spotted the error in the firmware. Although they're keeping the patch proprietary, I'm pretty sure I figured out the fix on my own."

Howie Boy's fogged mind had trouble understanding all the nerdspeak. "Can you translate that into plain English?"

Manty waved him off. "None of that matters. The cool thing is, while I tried duplicating the fix, I stumbled across a different vulnerability in their code, one I'm sure I can exploit."

When the nerd stopped talking, Howie Boy looked at him expectantly. "What exactly does that mean?"

Manty looked around one more time. "With a laptop and USB cable, I think I can break into any vault equipped with that particular model of lock."

Howie Boy felt his pulse quicken. "You mean you can rob banks?"

"Hypothetically, but I would never take a risk like that."

From the twinkle in Manty's eye, Howie Boy knew his pal had obviously been thinking along those lines. "If you don't plan on robbing a bank, how do you propose to test your theory?"

"The case study centered on a lockout incident that took place at the state convention center in Harrisburg. I was thinking of contacting the manufacturer and asking them if they could dispatch a technician to that site and have me ride along. If I could test my code on that vault and prove it works, I'd reveal the exploit to the company and easily earn an A on my research. I might even be able to land a job with them after graduation."

As an avid hunter, Howie Boy was aware the summer sports and outdoor show was scheduled that very week at the convention center. The show always drew a huge crowd. With a gate charge of twenty dollars a person and a fifteen dollar parking fee, their vault could hold a massive amount of cash.

He slid closer to Manty and draped an arm around his shoulder. "Drink up, Manty, I have an idea for an excellent adventure."

29

CHAPTER 29

Barlow and Irv tweaked their original plan. Given that Barlow was staying in Perry County to be with Pet while she recovered, he decided to embed himself with Les's crew and help on the New Bloomfield construction project. Irv's crew would finish up in Ohio and relocate to Pennsylvania for the winter. Barlow being there would ease the transition.

On Saturday morning, four days after Pet's accident, she was due to be discharged. Both her mother and Barlow waited at bedside for the nurse to arrive with a wheelchair to roll her out. Pet was dressed and argumentative. Her mother insisted she should stay with her for a few days, but Pet was digging in her heels, asserting she wanted to go to her own apartment.

"You need a few more days to recuperate," Mrs. Henning said. "It only makes sense that I help you with that."

Why wouldn't she want to spend a few days with her mother? He kept his mouth shut not wanting to get in the middle of it. Mother and daughter would have to work it out.

"Your car is totaled," her mother pointed out. "How are you going to get around?"

"Duh," Pet rolled her eyes, just like she used to back in middle school. Barlow found it endearing. She went on. "I'll just have to buy a replacement."

The doctors had performed surgery on her broken nose. Her nose and cheeks were an ugly shade of purple. Her eyes and forehead had a yellowish tint. The scar on her forehead seemed to be healing nicely. The surgeon did a great job making sure the scar would be barely noticeable. Barlow thanked God the rest of her body wasn't broken.

Pet stood and paced. She didn't have any problem being on her feet. "I don't know why we can't just leave. Pushing me out on a wheelchair is totally unnecessary."

"Honey, it's just standard procedure. Calm down."

Pet looked out the window. "Besides, Barlow wants to visit me every day after work, and my apartment is closer to the Dancing Bear than it is to your house. He wouldn't have to drive so far to see me."

Mrs. Henning went quiet. It appeared as if she was going to give in. She looked at him. "Barlow, why don't you come stay with us? It'll save you the cost of lodging."

Her request blindsided him. He said nothing while considering how to respond.

"When you were growing up, you spent as much time with us as you did at home. It wouldn't feel odd to me if you came to stay a while."

"Really, Mom? Are you serious?" Pet looked at Barlow. "I'd like that."

He decided he liked the idea too. "It would be convenient. I need to have a couple meetings with an auctioneer to dispose of Dad's house. It's next to yours, and I'd be right there. Pet, we could more easily work together on solving my mystery." He didn't want to get more specific, not knowing how much she had disclosed to her mother. "I could take you around shopping for a car."

"It would be nice having a man around the house again," Mrs. Henning said. "If only for a little while."

Pet met his gaze.

He grinned. "When you're all healed up, I'll help you get settled back into your apartment. Your mom is right about how much time I used to spend at your place. It'll be just like old times."

She looked at the floor. The corners of her mouth quivered. Barlow knew that look well, just like he knew everything else about her so well. She was holding back a smile.

Petronia regarded the bedroom that used to be hers while growing up. The old oak dresser and matching double bed held so many memories. She ran a hand across the quilt on her bed, a gift from her grandmother who was now long gone. Everything looked exactly the same as when she had been a teen, even the robin egg blue color of the walls. She had never been much into pink. Despite the lingering pain she suffered from her accident, being here spread a warm glow through her core.

She wondered how much of that warm glow could be due to Barlow taking up residence in the guest room on the other side of her wall.

Her soul filled with glee when Barlow told her about his breakup with Caroline. He had visited her every evening in the hospital, staying for hours, reminiscing, playing cards, watching the crappy hospital TV, and she reveled in the attention he showed her. She felt like a school girl again.

Could this actually be happening? The two of them coming back together? It seemed as if circumstances conspired to make it so. The unlikeliness of it all made her head spin. She needed to be careful, though. She wouldn't be able to endure the emotional trauma if he hurt her again.

She heard a gentle knock at her door. "Come in."

Barlow entered and looked all around. "What happened to the boy band posters you used to have plastered all over your walls?"

She recalled her obsession with the flash-in-the-pan music groups who burst into popularity one minute and then tended to disappear just as quickly. "Honestly, I don't know. I think Mom and Dad took them down while I was at university."

He regarded her. "How do you feel? Did the bumpy ride home cause your pain to flare up? Can I get you some hot tea and some aspirin?"

"I'm fine, Barlow. I appreciate your concern, but you don't have to baby me all the time."

He grinned. "Maybe just some of the time then."

"In that case, tea would be nice. What's my mother doing?"

"She's downstairs watching TV in the rec room. I think she wants to give us some privacy."

His observation amused her. "That's funny. When we were teens, Mom never left us alone for more than ten minutes at a time."

He chuckled. "That was her mistake. Back then, ten minutes was way more time than I needed."

Petronia could feel herself blushing. She threw a pillow at him. "Go fix my tea. I'll be right down."

After he left, she entered the bathroom and inspected her face in the mirror. She wanted to look nicer for him but realized no amount of makeup could hide the swelling. Barlow was definitely seeing her at her worst. She winced. This was way worse than the time she had that zit on the tip of her nose.

She joined Barlow in the kitchen and sat at the dinette while he heated a cup of water in the microwave. "Should we join Mom watching TV?"

Barlow frowned.

"Or, maybe not?"

The microwave dinged. Barlow removed the cup and dropped in a tea bag. He set the cup in front of her. "If you're up to it, I wanted to talk with you about our case."

His words sounded funny to her. "Our case? You talk like a cop."

"No, that would be you."

A bolt of anxiety shot through her. "I hope so. My tox screen came back negative, so there's no problem there, but the incident is still under review. There's still the question of how I managed to run off the road. Barlow, if another car happened to be coming around the curve, I could've killed someone."

He sat beside her. Their knees touched which made her go all warm inside.

"Don't beat yourself up. Until you get your memory back, you don't really know what happened."

Something was there just out of reach. "I have this sense that someone was following me, but it could be a false memory."

"Let it go. I want to talk with you about Howie Boy Collier."

What were the odds, Petronia wondered, that Irv from Ohio had known who the guy was when nobody local remembered him? She hadn't been much of a sports fan, but a lot of people around here were. She supposed college athletes were just like those boy bands from her youth, all the rage in one moment and then completely forgotten the next. "Yeah, go ahead. I'm listening."

Barlow cleared his throat. "While you were recuperating, I did a Google search. Turns out this guy is more popular than we imagined. He even has a Wikipedia page."

"No kidding!"

"Just like Irv said, he played football at Penn State University and graduated with a degree in marketing. He took a job with his father's company. You'll never guess who his father is."

Pet had no idea.

"Uriah Collier."

Hearing that name surprised her. "The Uriah Collier? The tycoon?"

"Yep. His father put him in charge of a land development company in Idaho. Howie Boy relocated right out of college and has lived there ever since. He's married to a Shoshone lady and has two kids, a boy and a girl."

Petronia sipped her tea. "It's amazing what a person can find out by doing a Google search. As cops, we find it just as useful as the official criminal databases we have access to."

"I haven't gotten to the juicy part yet."

She saw excitement in Barlow's eyes. "By all means, go on. Tell me more."

"A few years ago, the Colliers ran into some problems with mineral rights leases. Environmental concerns. Uriah decided to solve the problem by running his son for the Idaho state legislature. With his athletic good looks and having married a Native American woman, fathering two kids, championing blended families, he was an all-American poster boy and won his election bid. The environmental problems eventually went away."

Petronia scoffed. "No doubt his father's money had a lot to do with it."

"For sure. I also found out the family has deep political connections." Barlow sat back in his chair and wore a serious expression. "Because of his political success and connections, it's rumored that Howie Boy is about to announce an exploratory committee."

Her breath caught. "He has further political aspirations?"

"Howie Boy Collier is thinking about running for governor of Idaho."

30

Chapter 30

Barlow loved the way Pet lit up when he told her all the details he found out about Howie Boy Collier. Getting her mind off the accident worked like a tonic. Her mood improved, and she seemed eager to get to work on their case.

"One thing you never explained to me." Barlow removed the photo from his pocket. "How did you manage to get this?"

She squinted at the photo making her swollen eyes look even smaller. "The detective originally signed to the case gave it to me. Even though he had been ordered to turn everything over, he held onto this photo."

"Do you want another cup of tea?"

Pet glanced at the bottom of her cup. "No, thank you."

Barlow tapped his index finger against the photo. "Now that we know more, do you think he might want to join us to figure out what's going on?"

She shrugged. "Maybe. He's a school resource officer now, but this is the one case that he still carries in the back of his mind. Man's name is Custer Graham."

He picked up her empty tea cup and carried it to the sink. That name, Custer Graham, sounded familiar to him. When the reason why popped into his head, Barlow nearly dropped the cup. "Custer Graham is dead."

"What?"

Barlow shuffled back to the table and sat. "While you were recuperating in the hospital, his death was all over the local news. The man was murdered. The authorities speculate he got in the middle of a drug deal between two of his students."

The instant Barlow revealed Custer Graham had been murdered, Pet's memory returned as if someone lifted a veil from in front of her eyes. Chills danced the length of her spine as she put it all together. Unable to keep the panic from her voice, she said, "I have to leave and go into hiding. You and my mother are in danger being around me."

"Why?" Barlow asked.

"I didn't run off the road. I was pushed. Someone tried to kill me. They didn't succeed and are going to try again."

Barlow leaned forward and grasped both her arms. "Pet, you're shaking. Tell me what you're thinking."

"There's a leak. Somehow, word got back to the wrong people that I've been poking around in this case. They must know Custer Graham gave me that photo. They killed him and they tried to kill me. Don't you see, Barlow? Whoever these people are, they're getting rid of the loose ends."

"We're getting close to solving this thing," he said. "The Colliers are behind it. Who else could it be? They have the money and power to pull off something like this. What we don't know yet is why? What really happened that night? What is so important to cover up it would cause them to kill?"

"You already hit on the motive. Howie Boy has his eye set on politics. If word gets out he robbed the convention center and might be involved in the murder of Neil Mantener, he can kiss his political aspirations goodbye."

"Along with the political clout that can be leveraged to enrich his family businesses," Barlow added.

"I don't know what to do or who to trust. I can't take this information to my lieutenant."

"You don't trust him?"

She tamped down a rising panic. "I told him I was working a hobby case, but I never told him which one. I had a discussion with Trooper Morg Johansson about what it meant when a case was administratively closed, but I wasn't specific with him either. I don't think either one of them could be the leaker."

Barlow's expression took on a hardness she had never seen before. "Think, Pet, who else might have known? The attack on you happened too soon after we showed that photo around for them to have mobilized so quickly. It had to be someone who knew very early on what you were up to."

Pet mentally retraced her steps from the moment Barlow asked her to help. She was sure she hadn't spoken to anyone else. She never left any files out in the open or on her computer screen. She gasped. "The files! I contacted Troop H headquarters to see if there was anything in the original case file that hadn't been entered into the computer system. I spoke with a sergeant in the records department. I had to be fairly specific with him as to what I was looking for."

"Who?" Barlow asked.

The name came to her. "Tanzin. Sergeant Gus Tanzin. He has to be the leak."

"Can you go to your lieutenant with this?"

"He's seems like a good man, but I don't know who else Tanzin might have informed or who else might be in on it."

With her cop brain now fully focused, Pet saw a possible way out of her predicament, but it would take nerves of steel. The thought of what she needed to do frightened her, and she didn't know if she could carry out her plan. Her throat went dry, and she wished she had something stronger than tea.

"Tomorrow morning you and I are going to contact Tanzin," Barlow said.

"I was thinking the same thing. Except I'm law enforcement and have standing. You don't. You need to let me do this by myself. Alone."

Barlow reached across the space between them and rested a finger on her chin. He tilted her head so that they met each other's gazes. The determination she saw in his eyes and his words reassured her. "Not alone. I left you alone once before. That's never going to happen again. Not unless you're the one to tell me you want me out of your life."

"I never wanted you out of my life."

Barlow gave her a gentle kiss. The tingling sensation was a replay of their first kiss way back in middle school.

He pulled away. "You want to find out for sure if this Sergeant Tanzin is the source of the leak?"

It took Petronia a moment to refocus. "It's obvious to me he's the source of the leak."

Barlow looked puzzled. "So, what do we hope to accomplish by contacting him?"

"Fear is conquered by taking action. I'm going to take action."

"Against whom?"

"The people at the top. Barlow, I plan on going directly to the source of this problem and confront them on their home turf."

31

CHAPTER 31

Ten Years Ago (Part 2)

The song above referenced in this chapter: "Jenny, Jenny," by Tommy Tutone

Being August, the weather was too warm for them to wear hoodies, so Howie Boy and Manty tried to appear as average and non-descript as possible wearing plain baseball caps and dark clothing. The convention center crowd for the closing day of the summer sports and outdoor show was overwhelming, everyone shuffling elbow-to-elbow through the unending aisles of displays, exhibits, and vendors.

The place had to have raked in a mountain of cash, Howie Boy figured. As he and Manty were carried along with the throng, neither of them was interested in the frenzied activity. Instead, they studied security camera placement, emergency exits, and tried to find the location of the vault within the complex.

As they neared the food court, Manty poked him and pointed to a kiosk. They broke away from the crowd to have a look. The kiosk displayed a floor map with a layout typical of the kind found in shopping malls with a "You Are Here" label and arrow. Doing a quick scan of the layout, they discovered a balcony overlooking the main floor. The balcony showed three locations labeled as Security, First Aid, and Lost-and-Found.

Manty looked up toward the balcony. "The vault has to be somewhere up there."

"Let's check it out," Howie Boy said.

They rode the elevator to the balcony level. When the elevator doors opened, the first aid station faced them. All around them on the balcony level, security personnel, convention center employees, and attendees milled around. It was a busy place with a lot of distractions. Nobody paid them any attention.

Walking past first aid, they came upon the lost-and-found station fronted by a long counter. A couple employees manned the counter. Behind the counter, tables were setup with various articles of clothing. A little girl screaming for her daddy was being soothed by a matronly lady who was trying to get the little girl to say her name so they could make an announcement.

"Hold up," Manty said. He walked to the counter. Howie Boy followed behind wondering what he was about to do and hoping whatever it was wouldn't draw attention to them.

As they approached, Manty got the attention of one of the employees. "I lost my iPhone in the men's room. I set it down to wash my hands and must've walked out forgetting to pick it up."

The employee, a plump, forty something guy wearing a sport coat with sleeves too short asked, "An iPhone?"

"Yeah, a gold one."

"Let me check." The guy walked to the rear of the room and punched a code into a five-digit keypad.

Manty scoffed. "Did you see that? The code he punched in was one-three-five. That's the factory default. They never bothered to change it."

"That back room must be where they keep the valuable stuff," Howie Boy said. "Why do we care?"

"It might prove useful later."

The plump guy returned shaking his head. "Sorry. There's a droid back there, but no iPhone."

Manty sighed. "Oh, well, thanks for looking. I'll check back later in case someone turns it in."

As they continued walking, Howie Boy chuckled and said, "You're a pretty good actor."

Manty ignored him and pointed to several thick orange cables trailing from the suspended ceiling into a large room. The room was fronted by a windowless door with a ten-digit keypad. "The security center. My guess is all the camera feeds go into that room via those fiber cables."

"The most likely location for the vault," Howie Boy said.

They hung out acting as if they were texting. A few minutes later, a security guard approached with a carrier holding two coffees. They surreptitiously watched as the guard punched in the code: eight-six-seven-five-three-oh-nine.

Howie Boy giggled, "That's Jenny's number from the song."

Manty shook his head. "I can't believe this place. They are really lax. The guard made no attempt to hide that code from our view."

"I guess he couldn't while carrying the coffee."

"I've seen enough," Manty said. "Let's discuss our next move."

A few minutes later, the two of them entered the food court and ordered overpriced tacos and beer. They found a vacant table. Manty pulled off his backpack containing his laptop and set it on the seat beside him. They planned ahead of time how to get the backpack into the convention center. Attendees weren't allowed to carry anything inside, but Howie Boy made a call to his father. Uriah Collier used his contacts to score them a vendor's pass.

Howie Boy took a bite of his taco. The damn thing was soggy. "What do you think?"

Manty seemed preoccupied, staring off into the distance while eating. "I don't know. I believe we can pull it off, but do we really want to risk getting caught? We're in our senior year of college. It would ruin us."

"We aren't actually out to steal anything. We're just trying to find out if your override works." At least that's what he wanted Manty to think.

Manty gave him a look like he was a dumb ass. "You think the cops will buy that story if we get caught."

"Let's make sure we don't get caught." Howie Boy planned to pocket as much cash as he could. If things went wrong, he figured his father could pull strings and get him out of it. He was pumped. This was going to be one of those defining moments, something he'd be able to talk about the rest of his life. He didn't need the cash, but the challenge and getting away with it would be epic!

When Manty smiled, Howie Boy knew they were going through with it. "So, what's your plan, Manty?"

"The guard carried two cups of coffee. That means there are likely two people monitoring security cameras. Once the convention center closes at eight, my guess is they will go off duty. We need a place to hide at closing."

The nerd was smart. "Where can we hide?"

"The back room of lost-and-found. Did you see the hours of operation? The convention center closes at eight but lost-and-found closes an hour earlier at seven. We just need to make sure nobody is looking and sneak in."

"The door code is one-three-five," Howie Boy reminded him.

Manty winked. "Got it."

"What about security cameras. Any chance the guard monitoring those cameras will see us enter?"

"What if they do?" Manty paused to take a drink from his beer. "Lost-and-found employees are civilians and don't wear uniforms. If the guards happen to be watching that particular camera, they'll have no reason to question two guys entering the room. They'll assume we just forgot something and returned. I figure they won't be watching the balcony cameras anyway since it will be closing time. It'll be more important for them to monitor the exits, making sure nobody is ripping anything off."

Howie Boy thought it through and could see only one hitch. "The security cameras. Won't they be recording our movements, even if nobody is actively monitoring?"

"For sure, but I'll erase the recordings. The possibility exists that the feeds are backed up to the cloud in real time, so we'll have to keep our heads down and avoid looking at the cameras until I disable the system." Manty frowned. "I can't believe I let you talk me into doing this."

Maybe his buddy needed a few more ounces of liquid courage. Howie Boy set down his soggy taco and stood. "I'll buy you another beer. Relax. What could possibly go wrong?"

32

Chapter 32

Howie Boy Collier sat outside his father's office annoyed over having to wait for his father's meeting to end. He glanced at his Rolex and decided to give the old man five more minutes. If he didn't summon him by then, he would leave and head for the family hunting lodge in Perry County.

The second week of deer season was underway, Howie's favorite time to hunt. He always skipped the first week when too many yahoos were afield. This annual trip was a ritual, one he never missed out on. His father, once an avid deer hunter, could no longer see the sense in it. A waste of time, the old man had told him. That was okay with Howie Boy. He liked the solitude of having the lodge to himself. No father, no wife, no kids, and no bothersome constituents. Just him and nature. And his rifle.

The office door finally opened and his father shook hands with his guest. "Pleasure doing business with you," his father said.

The man gave him a deferential nod. "Likewise."

As soon as the man disappeared from view, his father's smiling face changed, transforming into a sneer of disapproval. That's the face Howie Boy was used to seeing, his father's default expression.

Uriah Collier beckoned him to enter by wiggling his index finger. "Hold all my calls, Sara," he ordered his personal assistant.

After Howie Boy entered the inner sanctum of his father's office, the man closed and locked the office door. Well, that was new. His father never locked the door in previous meetings. Something serious had to be afoot.

Howie Boy walked to his father's liquor cabinet and poured two fingers of bourbon from a decanter and dropped in two ice cubes. He turned to his father. "Do you want one?"

His father shook his head and walked to the window facing south toward the Philadelphia sports complex. He sighed.

"What's with all the melodrama, Father. First the locked door, then the sigh?"

His father turned to face him. "You better take a seat."

Howie Boy chose a sofa and plopped down onto the soft cushions. "That bad, eh?"

"Yesterday I received a telephone call from a man named Tanzin, a state trooper on my payroll. He put a woman on the line, a female trooper by the name of Henning who is not on my payroll. Shocked the hell out of me because Lionel told me he had killed her."

"It's not like Lionel to make mistakes."

"Forget about him. The problem is Trooper Henning knows everything."

Howie Boy swished the ice around in his glass. "Everything about what?"

"Everything about what happened ten years ago."

He laughed. "That's not possible."

"Exactly what I thought too, at first. She told me she's in possession of a photo showing both you and Neil Mantener in the security office of the convention center."

Howie Boy took a sip of bourbon, savoring the burn at the back of his tongue and throat. "I thought you dealt with all the evidence. That stuff should've been destroyed years ago."

"It was, to my knowledge. The original detective, Custer Graham, must have held out on us. Somehow this Trooper Henning got a hold of a photo."

"What else does Graham still have?"

"Nothing. He's dead."

Howie Boy took another sip. This one didn't burn as much since his tongue was now numb. "Lionel took care of that problem?"

"Yes."

"But not the lady cop?"

"Apparently not."

Howie Boy considered what his father had just told him. "Why does the lady cop even care? What's motivating her to look into that dead case?"

His father approached and took a seat on a matching sofa opposite him. "Howard, she says there was a witness."

Howie Boy hated when people called him Howard. He relished his nickname because the boy part of the moniker caused people to underestimate him. Also, it made him appear self-deprecating and folksy, something his constituents ate up. It made them think they could trust him.

Whenever his father called him Howard, he expressed his contempt by calling his father by his first name. "That's bullshit, Uriah. Nobody saw me that night. I was out of there before the cops arrived."

His father leaned in close and lowered his voice, as if someone might be listening. "If that's the case, why did Trooper Henning mention cash at the scene of the wreck?"

Howie Boy's blood turned cold. "How could she possibly know that? Get Lionel to finish the job."

"Can't. He's in the wind."

Howie Boy was through sipping. He downed the rest of his bourbon. "What does the lady cop want?"

"An audience with me."

"You think she wants to shake you down?"

His father shrugged. "If that's all, it's no big deal. I'll pay her whatever she wants. What worries me is she might be some idealistic do-gooder who actually wants to solve the case. She might want to get to you through me."

"She's a state employee. Can't you get the governor to apply pressure, like you did back then with the police?"

"Unfortunately, son, the governor from back then has term limited out. He's not the governor anymore, and I don't own the new guy. Not yet."

The bourbon roiled in Howie's stomach. If even a whiff of his involvement leaked to the media, his political career would be finished. "Where did you leave things with the lady cop?"

"I had no choice. I set up a meeting with her. She'll be here this afternoon at four."

A smile crossed Howie Boy's face. "Father, does she know I'm here? Does she have any idea about my annual visit?"

"If she does, she didn't find out from me."

"The stakes are too high to trust anyone else to deal with her. I'll handle this myself." He got up from the sofa and walked to the liquor cabinet, poured himself another two fingers. "I've silenced tougher people than some lady cop."

33

CHAPTER 33

During their teen years, Barlow and Pet made a game of sneaking off together, the goal being to not get caught. They never were. Either that, or Pet's parents looked the other way. Compared to his mother and father—especially his father—the Hennings were fairly liberal minded about such things.

As Barlow slept in the guest room next to Pet's, he thought about sneaking and wondered if she was also thinking about it. The chemistry between the two of them had definitely rekindled, but rebuilding a relationship took time. He had been the bad guy by leaving her and needed to regain her trust. He didn't want to spoil the second chance they had by doing something stupid.

For the moment, he was happy with being Pet's friend, protector, and chauffer. The morning after coming home from the hospital, he had driven Pet in his work van to the PA State Police Troop H headquarters in Harrisburg. She confronted Sergeant Gus Tanzin in the records department, threatened to turn him in over leaking information that resulted in the murder of the retired detective. She demanded he get Uriah Collier on the phone with the purpose of arranging an appointment to see the tycoon.

A bold plan for sure. Pet had made Barlow sit in the lobby while it all went down.

"He knew I had him dead to rights," Pet told him later. "He couldn't take the chance. Even the suspicion of his leaking info would end his career. His colleagues would make his life a living hell."

Tanzin had Collier's private office number and had gotten hold of the man right away. Barlow thought it particularly brazen of Pet to take the phone from Tanzin's hand and speak directly to the powerful mogul. After hearing her tell him the story, Barlow wished he could've been in the same room to witness it.

The day after the meeting with Tanzin, Barlow drove Pet to a four o'clock meeting with Uriah Collier in Philadelphia. Unlike the day before when she had been on her own turf at Troop H headquarters, this time she was entering the lion's den. They were arguing about it.

"Your plan is reckless," Barlow said as he exited the PA turnpike toll booth and merged onto the Schuylkill Expressway toward center city. "I don't like it."

"Acting fast keeps the old man off balance."

"I'm not leaving you alone. It won't be just him. Given his wealth and power, I imagine he has an entire security team, maybe even the guy who tried to kill you. There's no telling what he might do or how he's going to react."

"He won't try anything while I'm a guest in his office. Besides, he knows I have a witness. He's going to want to know your identity. That makes you my insurance, so you need to stay in the van."

Everything about the meeting made him uneasy. "I wish you had backup. Are you sure staying quiet about this to your superiors is a wise move?"

"Until I get a better feel for the situation, I won't know for sure whom I can trust."

Barlow gripped the steering wheel. "I should at least be in the building with you. Maybe down in the lobby."

Pet shook her head. "Too risky. If they get to you, we lose our leverage and the case disappears." She turned to him. "Look, Barlow, you've been my protector ever since we were kids. I'm glad to have you by my side, but I'm not a helpless girl anymore. I'm a law enforcement officer with skills. Trust me to take care of myself."

"You're training doesn't mean diddly squat being only one person against what might turn out to be an army."

"Uriah Collier doesn't know I'm acting alone. For all he knows, my entire department is aware of my visit." She pulled down the sun visor and inspected herself in the mirror. "How do I look?"

"Gorgeous, as always."

Pet scoffed. "Yeah, right."

"The truth? You look like someone beat the crap out of you. The swelling around your eyes is going down, but you're still all purple. Are you sure you're up to this? We can come back when you're healed up better."

She pushed the visor back up against the roof of the van. "Maybe Collier will take pity on me and tell me what we need to know."

Although Petronia displayed bravado in front of Barlow, a feeling of dread threatened to overwhelm her. She wasn't sure if she was up to the task of taking on Uriah Collier. The whole thing was a bluff, a fishing expedition. She had no definitive proof, but her gut told her he had hired someone to kill her. Barlow was right. Anything could happen. She would like nothing better than the reassurance of having him by her side, looking out for her, just like he had always done.

She wasn't at her best, and she should have waited until fully healed and reinstated, but she also knew they didn't have the luxury of time. This hastily arranged meeting was meant to put Collier on defense.

The man obviously wasn't going to admit to anything, but by presenting him with the evidence she had so far and threatening to move forward with it, maybe he would make a mistake and let something slip.

Thoughts of Barlow distracted her when she should be concentrating. Petronia had meant to use the two-hour drive to talk with him about their relationship. She desperately wanted to pick up where they had left off ten years ago.

Could they?

He had been acting super careful around her, probably not wanting to push things. But she was beginning to resent him treating her like some fragile China doll. Other than the short kiss two nights ago, he hadn't made any other romantic moves on her.

He couldn't hide his feelings though. She knew him too well, the way he looked at her, and his body language.

During the drive home, she would definitely start the conversation. They needed to air things out, and she wanted to let him know she was ready for more.

"We're here," Barlow said as he turned off the van's engine. He had driven them into a public parking garage beside the Collier main office complex and parked on the roof. High cirrus clouds painted stripes against the sky.

Petronia unlatched her seat belt, took a breath, and reached for the door handle.

Barlow laid a hand on her thigh, stopping her. "Let's test the app one more time."

As a precaution, Barlow had installed the Find-my-iPhone app on his phone so he could track her phone. The test worked perfectly. The location of her phone showed up as a blue dot on his screen.

"If I don't hear from you in a half-hour, I'm going to call your cell," he said. "If you don't answer, I will call the police. If you're in trouble, we need some sort of code word."

That made her giggle. "So melodramatic."

"I'm serious."

She decided to play along, anything to ease his anxiety. "Okay, how about I love you?"

"That's a phrase, not a word."

She tsked and opened her door. "Don't be so technical."

As she got out, she heard Barlow say, "Okay then. That's what I'll expect you to say: I love you."

She leaned in before closing her door. "I love you, too." She turned and walked toward the building's entrance.

The man at the security desk referred to a computer monitor after Petronia gave him her name. He issued her a visitor badge and told her to take the elevator all the way to the top. She approached the bank of elevators and pressed the call button. A few moments later, the door to one of the cars opened unleashing a stream of people.

Apparently four was quitting time and everyone was in a hurry to beat the Friday afternoon rush hour traffic. She was the only one to enter the car going up. That added to her feeling of unease. While the car ascended, Petronia straightened the blazer of her business suit and ran a hand through her short hair.

She mumbled, "Don't know why I bother. The way my face looks, I'm not exactly going to make a formidable first impression."

A chime sounded and the elevator car slowed. The doors slid open. She stepped off. Directly in front of her stood a set of double doors with no windows. Glancing around, she noticed the entire top floor was one giant office.

After taking a few calming breaths, Petronia raised her fist and knocked.

34

CHAPTER 34

Howie Boy received the call from security that his visitor was on the way up. Minutes later, he heard the timid knock on the office door. His father had been overly concerned about the situation, but he felt confident about being able to handle the lady cop.

He opened the office door.

The woman standing in front of him was nothing like he expected, and the sight of her momentarily threw him off balance. He had anticipated a uniformed, armed, serious-looking, matronly sort. This lady hardly fit that picture. First of all, she looked as if someone had punched her in the face. Her nose had obviously been broken, and it looked like she had undergone recent surgery to fix it. Her face was bruised and swollen.

Had Lionel done that to her?

She wore a navy-blue business suit, like a detective, instead of a trooper's uniform. She was fit, athletic, and it was too bad she dressed in slacks. He imagined she had killer legs. The short hair bob didn't do her any favors, but despite her hair length and the bruises to her face, he could see beneath the damage she was a fine looking woman. A few years younger than he was, maybe in her mid to late twenties.

Unless she carried a small gun in an ankle holster or one in her purse, she appeared to be unarmed.

She broke the silence. "You're Howard Collier."

If she had planned to piss him off from the start by calling him Howard, she had succeeded. "I'm Howie Boy, not Howard, and Mr. Collier to you."

She seemed to recover from the surprise of seeing him and flashed a badge in front of his face. "I'm Petronia Henning, Trooper Henning to you, or you can just call me ma'am."

He chuckled. Her attitude amused him. He beckoned with his arm toward the interior office. "Yes, Ma'am. Please, come on in. Have a seat. Can I offer you anything to drink? Looks like you could use one."

She walked past him, erect, confident, maybe acting a bit too confident as if she were putting on a show. She gazed around the room. "No, thank you." She settled onto one of the office sofas.

"Do you mind if I have a drink?" He had already forgotten her name and didn't wait for her to respond. He approached the liquor cabinet and fixed himself a bourbon. He sat opposite her.

She sat, one long leg crossed over the other. "I was expecting to meet with your father."

"I hope you're not disappointed."

"Not at all, since you're actually my person of interest. I thought you lived in Idaho. What brings you to Pennsylvania?"

He sipped his bourbon. "My annual hunting trip. Your timing is right, although whether it's good timing or bad timing depends on the point-of-view and the outcome of this meeting."

The trooper cocked her head. "Are you expecting a bad outcome?"

"Maybe." He paused. "For one of us."

A corner of her mouth twitched, a sign she might be more nervous than she wanted to appear. "Are you threatening me, Mr. Collier?"

He forced a smile. "Not at all. I just have the feeling you're going to be disappointed. You aren't going to find what you're looking for."

She raised an eyebrow. "Oh? What am I looking for?"

"Suppose you tell me."

From her purse, she pulled a photo and reached over to hand it to him. He took it from her and studied the image. Damn. Manty had been so sure he had disabled all the security cameras. "Looks like someone photo shopped my face onto someone else's body."

The lady cop scoffed. "Do you really want to play head games with me? You'll lose."

Howie Boy kept the smile pasted on his face. "What can I say? It's amazing the things one can do with software these days."

"If that's the case, where were you the night the convention center was robbed and when Neil Mantener had his accident?"

"Don't know this Mantener character or what you're talking about. When was the convention center robbed?"

"August fifteen. Ten years ago."

He laughed. "You have got to be kidding. I can't remember where I was ten days ago, much less ten years."

The lady cop uncrossed her legs and sat back against the sofa cushions. "Since you aren't going to tell me, suppose I tell you."

"Be my guest. Entertain me."

"You and Neil Mantener attended the summer sports and outdoor show at the convention center with the intent of committing robbery. Somehow, you hid until after closing. You found a way to disable the security cameras and enter the vault."

"Whoa!" Howie Boy exclaimed. "What am I? Some sort of Marvel superhero to be able to accomplish such impossible tasks?"

"Definitely not you," the lady cop said deadpan, "but Neil Mantener could've pulled it off. He was an electrical engineering student at Penn State. I checked with his professors. They told me he was a whiz kid, genius level, certainly someone knowledgeable enough to breach a security system and bank vault."

Howie Boy sipped his bourbon. Manty had been all that. "Suppose what you say is true. How did he break into the vault?"

She smirked. "I contacted the manufacturer. That particular model had a design flaw. The electronics had a bug which would sometimes prevent the locking mechanism from opening, even when the right sequence of numbers was entered into the keypad. The company came up with a fix. My guess is that Neil Mantener figured out how to gain access by exploiting that flaw."

The lady cop had done her homework too well. He downed the rest of his bourbon.

She went on. "After loading all the cash into the steamer trunk, the two of you could've easily walked right out and driven away. Nobody would stop you."

"Steamer trunk?" A chill ran along his spine. How did she know about the steamer trunk? His father mentioned she knew about the missing cash, but nobody except he and Manty were aware of that detail. She actually did have a witness! Howie Boy wanted to fix himself another drink but held back. It would make him appear to be nervous. He needed to stay focused.

She kept talking. "You drove away. I figure the two of you decided to stay off the major highways and take back roads, just in case. Late at night, it was dark, you took a wrong turn, got lost, ended up in a remote part of Perry County."

Her insight was unnerving him.

The lady cop leaned forward in her seat. "I'm not a deer hunter like you, but I love hiking the outdoors. Something my daddy taught me that I'm sure an experienced hunter like you already knows. He said if I ever got lost, find a creek and follow it downstream. That direction always eventually leads to civilization. Is that what you and Neil did after you got lost? Did you take the township road and follow the Juniata River downstream hoping to find your way out?"

He relaxed a little. Now she was off base. They hadn't gotten lost.

She went on. "A sudden turn took you by surprise and the car crashed into the river."

Howie Boy swallowed. "Very imaginative, but I haven't the slightest idea what you are talking about."

"Neil Mantener was injured. You found him lying on the river bank and dragged him into the water, held him under until he drowned and took all the money for yourself."

He laughed. "Pure speculation. Neil Mantener died behind the wheel when the car got submerged in the river."

"How do you know that? Earlier you told me you never heard of Neil Mantener."

Howie Boy got up and retreated to the liquor counter. She had caught him, and he needed to figure his next move. "You sure you don't want one?" A lame attempt to obfuscate. He fixed another drink. When he turned, the lady cop was no longer sitting.

He took a sip. "I didn't know Neil Mantener, but I heard of him. We both attended Penn State at the same time. News of his death spread all around campus."

She placed her hands on her hips. "It's the why I don't understand. You come from great wealth. Why would you even bother to commit robbery when all you needed to do was ask your father for money?"

He felt a bit of relief. The lady cop didn't have a motive. "Like you said, I didn't need the money. I wasn't there."

"Except there's that pesky photo putting you at the scene of the crime with Neil Mantener."

"Look, my father and I have enemies. I already told you someone doctored that photo to make me look bad. This is an attempt by one of my political opponents to discredit me. I'm considering running for governor of Idaho, you know?" He hated how his voice had suddenly become whiny.

"And the witness who saw the steamer trunk full of cash." Her tone was more forceful now. Confident. "The witness who pulled Neil Mantener from the car and revived him."

"Pure speculation. Fantasy."

The lady cop approached and got into his personal space. "The witness is what's going to hang you."

He was becoming unnerved again and was starting to believe her. "Who is your witness?"

"How did you manage to escape with all the money?"

"Who is your witness?" Howie Boy repeated in a threatening tone.

She flashed a cocky smile. "You'll meet the witness during your trial for murder. I have all the information I need for now. By the way, Mr. Collier, your guilt is written all over your face."

He grunted. "Speaking of faces, you're one to talk."

The lady cop rolled her eyes. "Let's not get petty." She turned and headed for the door. If she supposedly had him dead to rights, why didn't she arrest him right now?

"Hold up." He considered what it all meant and dashed toward her, got to the door the same time she did, and blocked her from turning the door handle.

"Get out of my way," she demanded.

The game had turned, Howie Boy knew, and he was in deep trouble. Throwing his full muscular bulk, honed from years of football weightlifting behind the blow, he gut-punched her.

The lady cop folded at the waist and immediately dropped to the floor. She rolled into a ball and vomited. He was back in control.

He got to his knees and searched her, just in case she had a small gun. Nothing. He checked her purse. Nothing more dangerous than a cell phone. He powered it off and pocketed it. It might come in useful later.

She continued to lay there, gasping and retching.

"I was going to jaw you but took pity. You suffered enough damage to your face."

She tried to look at him but her face screwed up in pain.

"You have your theories. I have one of my own. You aren't arresting me despite what you believe to be overwhelming evidence. You aren't wearing your trooper uniform. You're here alone and without a weapon. All of that leads me to believe you're acting on your own and in an unofficial capacity. I'm even willing to bet nobody knows you're here."

He paused to get a reaction. Her gasps had turned into panting and abject terror showed in her wide eyes. Good.

"You could suffer a fatal accident." He grinned. "Just like my buddy Manty did ten years ago."

Grabbing a desk lamp, he unplugged it from the wall, found a pair of scissors in his father's desk drawer, and cut a length of the electrical cord. He bound her wrists behind her back.

She spoke in a hoarse wheeze and through tears, "Plenty of people know I'm here. You can't get away with whatever you have planned for me."

Howie Boy helped her sit up on the floor. "Another theory of yours we can put to the test?"

From behind, he placed his hands under the lady cop's arms and lifted her to her feet. She screamed in pain. He drag-walked her to the far end of the office opposite the elevators.

To a back door.

A door leading to the roof.

35

CHAPTER 35

It felt as if a battering ram had blown out her entire midsection. How could anyone punch so hard? Petronia remembered he had been a muscular football player during his college years. No doubt he still worked out. She should've seen it coming. She had goaded him too aggressively and backed him into a corner.

Petronia knew she was in trouble. Howie Boy had tied her wrists and was marching her through a door, up a set of stairs. Where was he taking her?

A door opened and a cold wind blasted her face making her eyes water.

They were on the roof.

Oh, god, he was going to throw her over! The punch to her midsection had weakened her and made every breath feel like a knife jab. She didn't have enough air in her lungs to scream and tried a feeble shout, "Help!"

A hand closed over her mouth. "Shut up. Nobody can help you now."

His hand cut off her air. She was suffocating but in too much agony to resist. Dark spots swarmed in her vision. He dragged her. He tossed her onto a hard seat and removed his hand from her face. She gasped for air.

Two men engaged in a heated conversation, Howie Boy and someone else. She wasn't able to sit up to see.

"You're out of your mind. I can't be a party to this," the stranger shouted.

"You will do as you're damn well told. You're paid well enough."

"What are you going to do to this woman?"

"That's not your concern."

"When I get back, I'm going to speak with your father," the stranger said. "This is bullshit. I won't be party to a kidnapping."

"After you drop me and her, you can do whatever the hell you want. Let's get going."

Petronia heard a door latch. Were they in a vehicle? On the roof? She struggled and finally managed to sit upright. In front of her, the stranger and Howie Boy Collier wore headsets. She noticed an instrument panel and the whine of a turbine powering up.

Barlow heard the helicopter before he saw it. A powerful engine vibrated the building, sending ripples dancing on the surface of his coffee cup sitting in the console cup holder. From his parking spot on the roof of the public parking garage, he watched the bird lift smoothly from atop the Collier building.

Dread filled him. Although he knew it to be irrational, Barlow sensed Pet was aboard. He wished he had binoculars. During the next few seconds he'd have a clear view inside the cockpit, but it was too far for him to make out individuals with the naked eye.

He banged his hands against the steering wheel. "Damn it."

The helicopter rotated in mid-air and nosed due west, into the setting sun. The thing was fast. In a minute, it was a mere speck against the sky. A moment after that, it was gone.

Barlow punched the speed dial for Pet's cell phone. It went immediately to voice mail. "Where are you, Pet? I saw a chopper leave the Collier building. I hope you aren't aboard." He tried the Find-my-iPhone app. It displayed: "Offline." Why the hell had she turned off her phone?

Barlow exited his van and headed for the building main entrance. He entered through the revolving door and marched up to the security desk. "A lady state trooper named Petronia Henning came through here about half-an-hour ago. She had an appointment with Uriah Collier. Can you check to see if she's still with Mr. Collier?"

The attendant shot him an expressionless stare. "Are you with law enforcement?"

"No, I'm Trooper Henning's driver."

"Then, sir, I'm afraid I can't confirm any information with you. Mr. Collier's appointments are strictly confidential."

Barlow didn't have time to dance around with this man. "I'm only asking if you can check if Trooper Henning is still here. I believe she is in danger."

That got the attendant's attention. He pushed back on his chair and stood. "What kind of danger?"

"She was supposed to check in with me and didn't. A helicopter recently left the rooftop. I believe she may have been taken against her will."

The attendant smiled and spoke to Barlow as if he were a small child. "Sir, helicopters come and go from this rooftop all day long. There's no reason to suspect foul play based on that observation."

"Then why doesn't she answer her phone?"

"I really wouldn't know."

He wasn't going to get anywhere and decided to do something different. Barlow exited the revolving door and ran around the city block to the rear of the building. People streamed all around him appearing anxious to get home to start their weekend. He found what he was looking for, a loading dock. He slipped in without being questioned. Could he find the elevators before being noticed?

He slipped into a bathroom—luckily it was a single—and locked the door. He tried Pet's phone again. Still straight to voice mail. Adrenaline pumping, he found it hard to think. He needed to gain access to the penthouse office. That's where Pet was supposed to meet with Uriah Collier.

Elevators were usually located near the center of the building.

He opened the bathroom door and peeked. People were still walking out. Most were dressed in business suits so he would stick out in his casual clothes. He had to risk it.

Going against the flow of people leaving, he made his way deeper into the building. In the distance, he heard the chime of an elevator car as it opened onto the lobby. Rounding the corner, he stopped dead and reversed course, halted out of view of the security attendant he had spoken with. From where the man sat, he had a clear view of the bank of elevators.

Barlow knew he had to time things perfectly. He heard the chime of another elevator car. The door opened and people made their way past the attendant toward the building entrance. He stepped behind them and ducked into the elevator.

The doors seemed to take forever to close, but the attendant never looked his way. He breathed a sigh of relief and pressed the button for the top floor.

After a quick ride up, the elevator door slid open revealing a double office door. Should he knock? If Pet was still in there, it might disrupt things if he just barged in. On the other hand, she had turned off her phone.

He eased the door open, surprised it wasn't locked.

Inside the office, Barlow found a couple dirty drink glasses, a lamp on the floor missing its electric cord, and a pool of vomit.

His heart pounded at the ominous sight. "What happened here?"

He took a few minutes to explore and discovered the back door to the helipad on the roof.

More so than before, Barlow sensed Pet to be in grave danger. He made a hasty exit, desperate to return to his van.

36

CHAPTER 36

The disabling punch Howie Boy Collier had delivered to her torso incapacitated Petronia. The sharp pain in her liver wasn't a good sign, and she worried about internal injuries. She recovered enough during the helicopter flight to recognize the Harrisburg skyline and Harrisburg International Airport.

A Ford Explorer waited for the helicopter near a private terminal. Howie Boy helped her from the chopper. She groaned, barely able to breathe much less walk.

"Behave yourself, and I promise not to hit you again," Howie Boy told her.

She had no choice but to play along. One thing in her favor, this was her home turf and she knew the territory. As soon as he settled her into the backseat of the Explorer, Howie Boy pulled a black scarf from the glove box.

You'll need to wear this, doll." He tied the scarf around her eyes. "Don't take it off until I say so."

"Don't call me, doll." She wouldn't be able to take it off anyway. Her hands were still tied behind her back.

Pet heard the helicopter power up, likely on a return trip to the office tower in Philadelphia. She wondered if the pilot would report her abduction. Probably not. She heard the front door slam shut. Howie Boy started the engine.

"We're going to my family hunting lodge," he said. "I know you patrol Perry County, but I doubt if you've ever been to our lodge. It's very remote, way up in the mountains. The blindfold is precautionary. In the unlikely event you escape after we get there, you won't know which way to go."

Follow the water downstream, she thought. It would eventually lead to civilization. Apparently, Howie Boy hadn't been listening when she told him that back at his office. She found it encouraging, him making sure she wouldn't see where he was taking her. It meant he might not kill her right away.

"Only reason you're still breathing," he said, as if reading her mind, "you need to tell me who your witness is."

Petronia said nothing.

They drove for over an hour, the last ten minutes over a bumpy, rough road. She figured it was a dirt road or two-track up into the mountains. When the vehicle stopped, he let her out and unmasked her.

From the angle of the setting sun Petronia could determine they were on the north facing side of a mountain. The view was spectacular, if you liked seeing nothing but barren trees.

They had shed their leaves weeks ago. Behind her stood a grove of pines. In the middle of the grove, a large log home with a green metal roof and stone chimney. A covered porch wrapped around the front and sides.

"Nice place," she uttered through her pain.

"Glad you like it," Howie Boy said. "You'll likely be here a while."

He led her up a wide staircase, unlocked a massive front door with a skeleton key, and motioned for her to enter. He flicked on the lights. They stood in a great room, a stone fireplace on the interior of the wall opposite the stone chimney she had seen from the outside. The furniture was mostly made of polished wood covered with cushions; the motif of the place decidedly rustic.

It reminded her a lot of the Inn of the Dancing Bear.

"Can you untie me?" she asked. "I really need to use a bathroom."

He unfastened the electric cord that bound her. She rubbed her wrists to get the blood flowing.

"Bathroom is that way." He pointed.

Pet found herself in a small, windowless, powder room. She locked the door and removed her blazer and blouse. Her belly was painted dark purple, almost black. Not good. After relieving herself, she checked for blood in her urine and felt a small measure of relief when she found none. Still, the pain she was experiencing meant serious trouble. She redressed and left the powder room.

Howie Boy sat on a recliner, fully extended. He looked tired.

"What now?" she asked.

He met her gaze. "I don't rightly know. We're in uncharted waters."

"You could let me go. I'm in a lot of pain. Your punch hurt me really bad. I'm pretty sure I'm bleeding inside."

"Tell me about the witness, and I'll consider letting you go."

She sat on a sofa, the effort nearly bringing tears to her eyes. "Do you have any pain meds?"

Howie Boy got up and walked away. He appeared with a bottle of Bayer aspirin and a prescription vial of Oxycodone. He handed them both to her. "If you're bleeding, best not take the aspirin. Anyway, the oxy will be more effective. Let me get you a glass of water." He disappeared again.

Pet heard water running from the kitchen tap and wondered why he was being so hospitable. He returned and handed her the glass.

She downed two oxy tabs. "You seem to care about my comfort. Does that mean you're not going to kill me?"

He lowered himself back into the recliner. "I don't want to kill anyone. I'm not a monster, and I'm profoundly sorry about hitting you so hard. I had to stop you from leaving."

Pet didn't believe him. He was just being nice to find out about Barlow. "Yet here we are. You can't keep me forever."

"I know that. I'm thinking about my options."

"Just so you know, you're wrong about me being alone. There are people who know I had an appointment today. Then there is the security attendant in your lobby. Your father and his secretary whom I spoke with over the phone earlier also know. No matter what happens, if there's an inquiry, the truth will come out."

Howie Boy cradled his forehead in his palm. "Shut up. I need to think."

"I can help you to think. Kill me or not, it's over. I am a Pennsylvania State Police Trooper who has gone missing after making an appointment with your father. If I disappear everything will point back to your father and eventually to you. Let me take you in. Don't make this situation worse for yourself."

Howie Boy laid his head back against the recliner cushion and sighed. "I have a wife and children. I'm running for governor."

"I don't care about your politics."

"It's ruined," Howie Boy lamented, "all ruined due to a youthful indiscretion that happened long ago."

"Is that what you call killing Neil Mantener? A youthful indiscretion?"

He raised his voice, sounding manic. "I've atoned for Neil Mantener many times over. I've provided jobs to hundreds of families, I've built hospitals and schools." He got out of his chair and started pacing. "I can fix this. There's still time. I just need to think."

The man was panicking and talking in circles. Petronia didn't see the sense in continuing to argue. Besides, the oxy was kicking in, and she was having trouble keeping her eyes open.

"Let me help you to one of the guest bedrooms upstairs," he said. "It has its own bathroom, so you'll have privacy."

Petronia didn't want him to touch her. "I'll find it myself." Except she had trouble standing on her own.

He came to her side, gently raising her. "Like I said, I'm no monster. I don't want to hurt you...any more than I have to."

Too weak and in too much pain to respond, she couldn't resist his helping her up the stairs and into the bedroom. He guided her onto the bed and removed her shoes.

"Don't touch me," she protested.

He covered her with a blanket. "Why did you have to stick your nose in my business, doll? Why couldn't you just leave things be instead of putting me in the position of deciding if you should live or die?"

Because she was a good cop. He may have bought off others, but he wouldn't be able to buy her off.

"You don't look so good," he said. "You might be right. There's a good chance you have serious internal injuries." He leaned over her. "I'll make you a deal. Tell me who your witness is, and I'll take you to the hospital."

"No witness," she mumbled and closed her eyes. "I lied about that."

"You're lying now. I figure the only reason this long-buried case got reopened is because someone stepped forward. You told me about the steamer trunk and nobody knew about that. Someone saw me."

"No witness," she repeated barely conscious now, wanting desperately to escape her pain by falling asleep.

"If you're busted up inside, you might not survive until tomorrow. Tell me, and I'll drive you to the hospital immediately."

Petronia's mind drifted to Barlow. He had to be out of his mind wondering what happened. Did he love her enough to rescue her? Would he even know where to look? They had wasted ten of their best years apart. Now that they were coming back together, it wasn't fair that she should die.

"Come for me," she mumbled her plea. "Barlow."

Before sleep closed in on her, she heard Howie Boy Collier repeat the name she had just mumbled.

"Barlow."

37

CHAPTER 37

Ten Years Ago (Part 3)

The plan worked flawlessly, just as he and Manty had planned it. They hid in lost-and-found until eleven which was three hours after the convention center closed. They kept their heads down, away from the cameras, and punched in the code to enter the security suite. Howie Boy found the lights and flicked them on.

In front of them sat a desk ringed with monitors, all of them dark.

Howie Boy sighed in relief. "Everything is turned off. We didn't have to worry about keeping our heads down."

Manty quickly walked over to a computer tower. "That's not so. The monitors are turned off, but the cameras are still recording." He pointed to a console having so many tentacle-like cables attached, it looked like a mutant octopus. The cooling fans in the console hummed. "Each one of these cables is attached to a camera somewhere in the facility."

That dismayed Howie Boy. "It'll take us all night to disconnect them all."

Tracing a cable from the rear of the console, Manty followed it into a conduit that ran up the wall, across the ceiling, and into a breaker box. He opened the box, studied it for a moment and pulled a switch. The humming stopped. "Now, it's turned off. All cameras are deactivated."

"Way to go, Manty." Howie Boy looked around for the vault.

From his backpack, Manty pulled a toolkit. He opened it and removed a screwdriver. Next, he started taking apart the computer case.

"What are you doing?"

"I need to remove the drives from the computer to destroy the recordings."

"Can you tell if the recordings are being backed up?"

Manty continued to work on the computer case without looking up. "The computer tower is attached to the Internet so it's possible, but I doubt it. This system isn't as sophisticated as I thought it would be."

"Lucky for us."

A few minutes later, Manty had all the drives removed and stuffed into his backpack. He smiled. "And now for the main event."

The vault was built-in to a block wall with a steel door about eight feet tall by four feet wide. The locking mechanism looked like a six-inch diameter, disk shaped key pad.

"Oh, baby, baby." Manty pulled the laptop from his case and powered it on. After it booted up, he attached a cable to the interface on the bottom of the lock. He looked at Howie Boy. "Here goes."

Howie Boy clenched and unclenched his fists in nervous anticipation as Manty worked the keyboard. When Manty frowned, he thought it wasn't going to work. He kept at it. Five minutes passed, then ten. "What's the hold up?"

"Shut up. I'm almost there and need to concentrate."

He didn't like being told to shut up, especially by a twerp like Manty. He decided to overlook the slight this time. Another five minutes passed and Howie Boy started getting nervous. "We've been here a long time."

"I know that," Manty snapped. "Let me work." His fingers danced across the keyboard until he abruptly stopped, his finger poised over the enter key.

"Well?" Howie Boy had lost his patience.

Manty pressed the enter key. "Voila." A sound like thunk came from the vault door. He pumped his fist in the air. "Yes!"

Howie Boy didn't take the time to celebrate, he grabbed the handle and pulled the door open. He heard Manty gasp.

He peered into the vault and was stunned at the sight of row upon row of bundled cash. "Whoa."

Manty cheered. "The exploit exists. I proved it."

Sitting near the vault was a trunk. Howie Boy figured it would be perfect. He opened the top and found it loaded with video equipment. He upended the trunk and dumped the equipment.

"What are you doing?" Manty asked.

"We're going to stuff this trunk with as much cash as it can hold."

Manty stood in front of the entrance to the vault. "Hold on. We just did this for the thrill of it and to see if my code would work. Stealing money wasn't part of the plan."

Howie Boy shoved Manty out of the way and entered the vault dragging the trunk behind him. "The plan has changed."

"You're nuts. We can't do this."

Howie Boy laughed maniacally. "Management of this place are a bunch of fools. I figured they would've taken all this to the bank after closing. I thought we might find a thousand or two at most." He grabbed a stack of bills and tossed it into the air. "Look at it fly! Their mistake is our gain."

Manty stood, back straight, arms folded across his chest. "I can't let you do this."

"Do you think you're man enough to stop me?" He outweighed the nerd by fifty pounds, all of it muscle from weightlifting and getting into shape for football season.

Manty persisted. "Think it through. Taking this cash would be the same as declaring war. The cops will never stop looking for us."

The combination of adrenaline rush, excitement, and joy surpassed anything Howie Boy ever experienced before. It was better than sex! It was as if he had come to life for the first time. He pulled Manty into the vault with him. "Start stuffing this trunk."

With a defeated look on his face, Manty said nothing else and did what he was told. The two of them shoveled piles of cash into the trunk until it overflowed. Howie Boy closed the top and secured the latches, but the latch on the left side wouldn't stay closed.

"It's bulging," Manty said. "We have to take out some of the cash to get it to latch."

"Bullshit, we're taking it as it is."

Manty fussed over relocking the vault and closing and locking the door to the security suite. "They'll find out soon enough they've been robbed, but let's not make it so obvious for them to find out right away."

With a man on each end of the trunk, they carried it to the balcony elevator. On the ride down, Manty said, "We need to be careful about the parking lot in case there's a guard lurking around out there somewhere."

They managed to get the trunk out and into Manty's sedan without being detected. They had decided on using Manty's vehicle, because his older sedan was non-descript and blended in. Howie Boy's SUV was big, flashy, and more memorable. Howie Boy had second thoughts about it now, wishing he were the one behind the wheel. "Get us out of here. Take it nice and slow."

The next step in the plan was to drive to his dad's hunting lodge in Perry County. From there, they'd split the cash. "Turn left at the signal light when you exit the parking lot. We'll take the interstate and head west."

While they waited for the light to turn green, a state police prowl car pulled up to the light and slowed when it turned yellow.

"Oh shit," Manty mumbled.

"Stay calm. He has no reason to suspect anything."

The light turned green and Manty made his turn onto the thoroughfare leading to the interstate highway. He kept glancing in the rearview mirror.

"Relax," Howie Boy said.

"The cop has a green light now. He's right behind us."

"Relax," Howie Boy said again.

"What'll we do if he pulls us over?"

"He has no reason to. Just keep to the speed limit."

"There's a trunk full of cash in the back seat. What if he asks us what's in the trunk?"

Manty's whining annoyed Howie Boy. "Get a grip. A cop car following us is a coincidence. The entrance ramp to the interstate is just ahead. The cop will likely get on there. Change of plan. We'll avoid the interstate and keep to this road and cross the river upstream. Then we'll exit at Millerstown. I know an alternate route."

The prowl car did not take the ramp onto the interstate and remained behind them.

"What do we do now?" Manty was so nervous his voice sounded high like a little girl.

Although he wouldn't admit it, Howie Boy experienced a pang of nervousness too. "Just keep going. We're just tooling along, minding our own business. That cop has no probable cause."

As soon as Howie Boy finished his sentence, the prowl car pulled closer behind them, lights flashing.

38

CHAPTER 38

Philadelphia rush hour traffic on Friday afternoon was a nightmare. Barlow inched his way north toward the PA turnpike. The traffic wasn't his only frustration. The Find-My-iPhone app for Pet's phone continued to display: Offline.

"Why did you turn off your phone?" After mulling over in his head what to do, Barlow concluded the most likely scenario was Pet had been on the helicopter. If she had gone willingly, she would have called him. That meant Uriah Collier had taken her. But where? What had gone wrong during the meeting?

After inspecting Collier's office, Barlow figured he had three choices. He could call the police, he could sit in the van and wait, or he could return to Pet's mother's house. Calling the police didn't seem to be a good option yet. He would have to divulge everything. Could he trust word wouldn't somehow get back to the people responsible for shutting down the case? That could make things worse for Pet.

Sitting in the van was also out. No way could he remain idle, hoping that Pet would contact him.

He decided to drive. The helicopter had taken a flight path due west, the same direction as Perry County. He hoped that sooner or later Pet would call or text. When that happened, he wanted to be out of the city and closer to her location.

Then there was the issue of Mrs. Henning, Pet's mother. If he arrived back at the house without her, how could he explain it? He might be able to get away with not returning until the morning. She would assume the two of them had stayed over somewhere, but wouldn't it be out of character for Pet to not call and tell her?

Maybe not. Barlow got the vibe that Mrs. Henning had been secretly hoping he and her daughter would become a couple again. Maybe she would interpret Pet's silence as progress being made in that direction. It might give her second thoughts about calling Pet's phone, because she wouldn't want to interrupt what might possibly be happening. Maybe if she did call and it went to voice mail, Mrs. Henning would think Pet didn't want to be disturbed while with him.

Maybe pigs would someday fly.

Barlow squeezed the steering wheel. The uncertainty of it all made his gut churn. Traffic crept along. How could anybody deal with a commute like this every day?

By the time he reached the turnpike entrance, the last rays of afternoon sun were fading. The traffic had thinned, so Barlow could finally make time. He hated the idea of stopping, but about half way back to Perry County he needed a rest room. He pulled into a service plaza for a quick pit stop and decided to also order a large coffee. It could end up being a long night.

Getting back into his van, Barlow set the coffee in the console cup holder and closed his eyes. While in the Marines, he hadn't been involved in many combat situations. Being stationed in a hostile country, though, always left him feeling edgy. Not scared, just anxious. What Barlow felt now was fear. If something happened to Pet, he wouldn't know how to go on. He would never get over the guilt of allowing her to enter that office building alone, even though she had insisted on doing so.

When his phone chimed, Barlow opened his eyes and stopped breathing. Pet's phone had come back online. The Find-My-iPhone app displayed a remote area of Perry County, the flashing blue dot showing the location of Pet's phone.

His phone rang. The caller ID showed Pet, and Barlow never felt more relieved.

He accepted the call. "Hello, Pet?"

From the other end of the line, he was greeted with silence.

After putting the lady cop to bed, Howie Boy poured himself a drink and sat in his favorite recliner. Before zoning out, she had uttered the name: Barlow. Could that Barlow person be her witness? Might just as easily be her husband, except she didn't wear a ring. A boyfriend? Her brother? At the moment, it didn't matter.

He took a few swallows of the bourbon, always relishing the warmth as the elixir trailed down his throat and into his stomach. Too much would make him foggy, but just a little always made him see things more clearly. He needed to come up with a plan. Right now. The lady cop would soon be missed, and he needed to resolve things.

After giving careful consideration to all of the possibilities, Howie Boy concluded there was no other way. He would have to kill her.

That saddened him. She was young and pretty, smart and brave too. What a waste. She might swear on a stack of bibles that she'd never report him. Of course, the moment he let her go, that's exactly what she would do. In spite of everything, she was still a dedicated cop.

The witness would have to die too. He needed to tie up all loose ends once and for all. Nothing could stand in the way of his bid to become governor. Too many of his constituents would benefit. So many things he could fix in his state, and who knew? After a couple successful terms as governor, he could set his sight on the presidency. His dream of getting back at those NFL assholes would come to fruition.

What was it that Spock espoused to Kirk? The needs of the many outweighed the needs of the few. The lady cop and her witness had to go. Howie Boy raised his glass toward her upstairs bedroom. "Sorry, doll."

The helicopter pilot, his father had in his pocket. That man would soon forget about the unwilling passenger. His father's secretary was aware of the appointment. She would assume the lady had come and gone. That would be his story too, if anyone asked. The lady came, asked a few questions, and left. How was Howie Boy to know what happened to her after she left?

The situation could be managed. He could make it work. The only person missing was the witness. After doing the deed, he might even get in a little deer hunting.

Tomorrow morning, at first light, he would fire up the backhoe and dig a hole. His father and Lionel had buried bodies here in the middle of these hundreds of acres. They always kept the backhoe gassed up for occasions such as this one.

Howie Boy swished the ice in his now empty glass. He had his plan, so he decided to fix himself another drink before tackling the Barlow situation. After pouring himself another, he pulled the cop lady's cell phone from his pocket and powered it on. Maybe she'd have Barlow in her list of contacts.

An alert message popped up on her display screen. One voice mail message from someone labeled Barlow Jackson. He played it: "Where are you, Pet? I saw a chopper leave the Collier building. I hope you aren't aboard."

Could Barlow be her witness? He pressed the recall icon. After two rings, someone answered, "Hello, Pet?"

At first, Howie Boy didn't know what to say. Pet? He hadn't bothered to remember the lady cop's name and had forgotten it two seconds after she had told him, but he was sure her name hadn't been Pet.

The voice at the other end asked, "Pet, is that you? Where are you?"

Howie Boy figured if he didn't respond, the guy might end the call. "Is this Barlow?"

A pause. "Who is this?"

Annoyed, Howie Boy said, "I believe I asked first."

"You're calling from Petronia Henning's phone. Am I'm speaking with Uriah Collier?"

It took Howie Boy a second to put it together. The lady cop—Petronia was her name—had made the appointment with his father. Barlow wouldn't know about the change in plan. Could he use that to his advantage? If things turned sour, his father would take the fall. "Yes, this is Uriah, but that's Mr. Collier to you."

"Yeah, whatever, let me speak with her."

"Whoa, not so fast," Howie Boy said, trying to do his best imitation of his father. "I have a few questions for you first."

"I drove Pet to Philadelphia this afternoon to meet with you. Why did you take her?"

"I needed to find out about you. What do you know about what happened ten years ago?"

Silence from the other end confirmed that Barlow Jackson was the mystery witness. If he wasn't, he would've responded with, "I don't know what you're talking about," or something similar.

"Ten years ago, I pulled Neil Mantener from his crashed car, left him on the river bank, and went for help."

"Who is Neil Mantener?" Howie Boy played along.

"And I saw a steamer trunk loaded with cash," Barlow continued. "Now, let me speak with Pet."

Bingo. Barlow definitely was the witness. "Don't worry. Pet is alive, but she's a bit indisposed at the moment. She's sleeping."

"Wake her."

Howie Boy chuckled. "Who is she to you? More than a cop, I take it. Someone near and dear perhaps?"

"Yes."

"In that case, I'm sure you'd like to see her."

"Name the place and time. I'll be there."

Howie Boy took a moment to think. He would ambush the man, kill him, and bring his body back to the lodge. Then he'd do the lady cop and bury the two of them together. "Are you familiar with The Inn of the Dancing Bear?"

"Yes, I know the place well."

"Meet us in the parking lot tomorrow morning at six. I'll hand Pet over to you at that time and answer all your questions."

"I'll be there," Barlow said.

Howie Boy ended the call and laughed. Stupid yahoo. He'd never see him coming.

39

CHAPTER 39

Ten Years Ago (Part 4)

"Oh shit," Manty squealed as the police prowl car followed, lights flashing. "What should I do?"

If they had taken his SUV and if he were driving, Howie Boy figured he would make a break for it and try to outrun the cop. With Manty being such a pussy and in his little four-cylinder sedan, they didn't stand a chance. "Only one thing to do. Pull over. You probably just have a taillight out or something."

Manty used his turn signal and drifted to the side of the road. Instead of pulling in behind them, the cop sped by.

Howie Boy laughed and sputtered, "He wasn't after us. What a rush!"

Manty gripped the steering wheel, breathing heavily. "I'm glad you enjoyed that. I damn near had a coronary."

"Nothing to worry about, he wasn't after us. Keep driving, I'll tell you when to exit."

They drove on. Manty's non-stop complaining grated on Howie Boy's nerves.

"With this amount of cash missing, the police are going to pull out all the stops," Manty argued. "They'll keep investigating until they find us. We might not be on video, but someone will remember something. Maybe the guys in lost-and-found will think we acted suspiciously, or maybe the security guard with the carrier of coffee will recall us lurking over his shoulder—"

"—Maybe the sky will fall," Howie Boy interrupted. "Look, there are no worries. We got away with it. Besides, what if someone does remember us? What are the cops going to be able to do with that information? There are thousands of guys who look like us who attended that show."

Manty said nothing for a long time. Howie Boy also kept quiet until they reached their exit. "Get off here at Millerstown. Turn right at the stop sign, then left when we get to the square in town."

After they executed the two turns and crossed the Juniata River, Howie Boy thought Manty had finally calmed down. They drove on for a while until the nerd opened his mouth again.

With only one hand on the wheel, Manty gestured with his other hand. "You know what I don't understand? Your family is wealthy. You have all the money in the world. What does this cash mean to you? Why are you insisting on taking such a risk in keeping it?"

An interesting question. For once, Howie Boy didn't feel irritated Manty had asked and actually wanted to explain. "You're right. It really isn't about the money. It's about the thrill of having done something so epic. Don't you feel alive right now? No drug high can compare to this."

"Right, we won't feel so alive when we get caught."

Howie Boy laughed. "There you go again. We aren't going to get caught. Think about it. With this cash, you'll be able to pay off all your student loans. The convention center just provided you with a free college education. You should be happy."

A few beats later, Manty spoke up. "Are you really going to let me keep half?"

"Of course. We're equal partners."

"And you don't care what I do with my half?"

"Why should I?"

Manty made a sudden hard left onto a side road almost crashing into a kid's school bus shelter. Howie Boy was thrown against the passenger door. "What the hell are you doing? I didn't tell you to turn here."

"I'm looking for a driveway or a turn around."

"What for?"

"I'm taking my half back."

The nerd's stubbornness and stupidity drove Howie Boy past the limit of his patience. "Pull over."

Manty shot a glance his way. "Why?"

"Because I'm kicking you out and taking your car. If you're going to be such a dumb ass, you don't deserve any of this cash."

When Manty didn't do what he asked, Howie Boy reached over and grabbed the wheel. "I said to pull over."

The two men struggled, fighting for control of the car. Howie Boy saw the curve in the road too late. "Watch out, asshole!" He scrabbled for the door handle and jumped out as the car skidded off the roadway and plunged down an embankment.

Howie Boy opened his eyes and saw the full moon. Feeling confused, he lay flat on his back. "I must've blacked out for a little while. Where am I?"

It slowly came to him. Manty, the stupid twerp had run off the road. He sat and checked himself. Nothing seemed to be broken. He must've hit his head when he jumped from the car. How long had he been out? What happened to the cash? He stood and took a deep breath, felt in his pocket for his cell phone. To his relief, it wasn't busted, and he had a decent signal.

Good thing the moon was shining; it made finding his way easier. Taking care not to fall on his ass, he descended the bank and heard the rushing water from the river. He started to panic at the thought that Manty might have miraculously found a way to get back on the road, leaving him stuck out here in the sticks. Then he saw the moon reflecting off the ripples in the night and the car's rear window.

The damn thing had taken a nose dive into the river.

He heard coughing. Following the sound, he discovered the nerd sitting on the bank. The fool must've swum free. "Hey, are you alright?"

"This doesn't change anything," Manty said. "The money has to go back."

A wave of anger crept up Howie Boy's chest and into his face. He grabbed Manty by the collar and hoisted him to his feet. "Listen to me, dick wad, because we aren't having this conversation again. We're keeping the cash, and I don't want to hear another word about it."

Manty wheezed and spoke. "It's over, Howie Boy. I'm going to the police. I'm going to tell them everything."

Something inside Howie Boy snapped. He went stone cold. Acting on animal instinct, he grabbed Manty in a choke hold and dragged him down the bank and into the river. "I tried being reasonable with you," he shouted. "I was willing to let you keep your share. Why did you have to be such an asshole?"

He plunged the smaller, weaker man face first into the current. Manty struggled, but he stood no chance against the rage working within Howie Boy. A minute later, it was over.

Feeling no remorse, he wedged the lifeless corpse into the driver seat and buckled him in, staging the scene and making sure the nerd's head stayed submerged.

A great deal of cash had floated out of the sprung open trunk and got carried away in the current. He spoke to the corpse. "No big deal. That was your half."

Howie Boy secured the steamer trunk and managed to drag it free of the car and up the bank. He rested for a moment to get his bearings. He needed someplace to hide until someone could come for him. That's when he remembered the kid's bus shelter. It would do nicely.

Slogging along with his water-soaked clothing, he half carried, half drug the trunk the rest of the way up the bank. The racket made by dragging the trunk along the road surface spooked him. Too much noise. Being August, the shoulder of the road was lush with weeds. He kept the trunk in the weeds which made the going tougher, but a lot quieter.

The high he experienced earlier at the thrill over stealing the cash returned when he reached the bus shelter. Howie Boy hid the trunk within the shelter and plopped onto one of the benches.

He stifled laughter after realizing not only was he going to get away with stealing the cash, he was also going to get away with murder. If he could get away with all that, nothing could stop him. Someday, he would make those NFL pricks pay for snubbing him. Quickest way to do that would be to become a politician. It would give him the power to make their lives miserable.

Howie Boy pulled his cell phone and punched in his father's number. "Hello, Dad," he said when his father answered. "I need you to send someone for me."

40

CHAPTER 40

Just about everyone knew smart phones could be tracked by law enforcement using the built-in GPS app. Howie Boy Collier had been wise to power off Pet's phone immediately after their conversation. What the man hadn't figured on was the active Find-my-iPhone app. Thanks to Barlow's foresight, the exact location now displayed on his screen.

He enlarged the scale and studied the image. The blue dot appeared on a Perry County mountainside in the middle of nowhere. "Where the heck was that location?" The nearest road was two miles away.

Had they hiked up a mountain? That made little sense. He guessed they had driven up a private access road not displayed on the map. Barlow realized he now had an advantage. Collier expected to meet him just after sunrise. He wasn't going to wait until then. He planned to use the cover of darkness to sneak to the location, hopefully find Pet, and get her away from danger.

As the evening wore on, the traffic became lighter and Barlow made good time. He arrived in Perry County just after eleven and drove slowly down the state road looking for an access leading up the mountain. In time, he realized he had driven too far and turned around. Overcast skies threatening snow left the night black, only the van's headlights illuminated the way.

After completing a second pass, Barlow grew despondent. Could he have been wrong? Could they have actually walked into the woods and up the mountain? Why would they do that? If so, wouldn't he find a parked vehicle somewhere along the road?

Then he wondered if an access road merged onto a different thoroughfare. Studying the display, he realized how unlikely that would be as the only other nearby road lay on the other side of the mountain.

Barlow turned around and tried a third time, crawling along at less than ten miles-per-hour. He didn't have to be concerned about obstructing anyone, because there was hardly any traffic on the rural road, especially at this hour. He almost missed it again. Tire tracks in the mud on the road's shoulder led to a nearly invisible cutoff. He eased onto the rough, unimproved road and stopped.

The blue dot blinked about two miles from his present location. Barlow had no idea if there was a direct line-of-sight from where Pet was being held. Collier and any other henchmen with him might detect his vehicle from far off. He also didn't know how far the sound from his motor would carry.

Knowing that the mountains were thick with trees—although the leaves were down—he decided to risk driving in halfway, about one mile. He'd find a place to park and then go on foot the rest of the way.

He drove at a snail's pace bouncing over every rocky bump. The construction van wasn't built for this kind of road, and he needed to be careful to not bottom out and puncture the oil pan. To Barlow's dismay, he realized the tree lined access road had no shoulder. There would be no place to park and no way to turn around.

For a moment, he experienced doubt. Barlow stopped driving. He was headed into unfamiliar territory at night with absolutely no weapon or even a solid plan. Pet needed him, so he could not screw this up. He wasn't going to allow anything bad happen to her. Barlow wished he had his Marine rifle. That reminder made him smile. He would rely on his training and his skills. Nobody was more adaptable to an unknown situation than a United States Marine.

Oorah!

He resumed driving, creeping along. Feeling tense as he drew ever-closer to the blue dot on his display, Barlow switched off his headlights.

He couldn't see a thing. That wasn't going to work. He didn't dare continue with his lights on. If there was any kind of security guard, he would be spotted. Barlow decided on his only other alternative. He pulled the van as far off the side of the lane as possible, his passenger door butting up against a tree trunk. Enough room remained that another vehicle might be able to squeeze by providing it wasn't too wide.

Of course, if another vehicle happened upon his van, he'd be screwed. It was a bad situation, but Barlow was willing to risk everything for Pet. He shut down the motor and scrounged around in the back of the van for the tire iron. Holding the two-foot-long, cold rod of steel gave him a measure of comfort. At least it was something. He also found his heavy work jacket and black wool cap. The mountain air was freezing, and it had started to snow.

He exited the van and eased shut the door. Groping along in the darkness, Barlow managed to stay on the lane. The amount of time it took for him to make forward progress seemed interminable until he finally reached a clearing. The display showed the blue dot to be within a hundred meters.

In the distance, he saw a glow of lights from inside a structure. It gave him hope.

Snow came down in big flakes, and he had no idea how extensive the storm would be. He cursed himself for not having listened to a weather report on the radio during the long drive. Sticking to the edge of the clearing, he decided to circle the house hoping to gain at least a minimal amount of reconnaissance. He might be able to detect anyone on lookout. It would be game over, though, if a lookout wore night vision gear.

The house loomed large with a big footprint, two stories with a light glowing from a second-floor room. There appeared to be no security, although hidden trail cams remained a possibility. More than likely, there was nobody actively watching the exterior for intruders. Why should they? Nobody had reason to expect a visitor way out here in such a remote location, especially on a cold, snowy night.

In the dim glow of lamplight, Barlow detected the silhouette of a vehicle and decided to take a closer look. Leaving the cover of the trees, he belly crawled along the ground, just like he had learned as a soldier. Keeping the vehicle between him and the house, he got to his feet and felt the hood over the motor.

Cold. They had been here for some time. In the absence of any other vehicles, he deduced there weren't many of them. Uriah Collier, Pet, and maybe one or two others at most.

Doable.

He crawled from the vehicle to the side of the house and stood. Listened. Not a sound. Falling snow seemed to always be accompanied by an eerie silence. Creeping around the house, sticking close to the wall, Barlow found a set of Bilco basement doors. He felt around and discovered the doors were secured with a heavy padlock. He might be able to break-in using the tire iron as a pry bar, but it would be noisy. He'd try that only as a last resort.

Bilco style basement doors

Barlow shivered. The snow fell harder now and was starting to lay. He continued his trip around the house until he reached the side of the front porch. Lattice work covered the gap between the porch and ground. At this spot, the covering had splintered and broken. He could easily squeeze through and hide beneath the porch.

He made a mental note about the damaged lattice and moved on. Barlow could discover no other point of ingress, unless there was a back door on the other side of the porch. He debated with himself and decided to go for it. He carefully climbed the steps, keeping to the edge where they would least likely squeak until he stood on the porch.

Everything remained silent.

Approaching one of the lit windows, he eased around until one of his eyes was able to peek inside. A man lay sprawled on a recliner, dozing. He was young. This couldn't be Uriah Collier, a man supposedly in his late seventies. Who was this? A bodyguard? Was he the only one? It dawned on him. This could be his son, Howie Boy. Except he was supposed to be living in Idaho. He'd be able to identify Howie Boy from the photo but couldn't be sure unless he got a closer look.

Where was the old man, Uriah Collier? Where was Pet? If Pet was his captive, he would lock her in the basement. That made him think again of the Bilco doors. Unless there was another way, he would have to reconsider breaking the lock. Before leaving the porch, Barlow decided to try the front door. One never knew, right?

He eased his way over. The knob was the kind you pressed down on with your thumb. Ever so gently, he gave it a try.

Locked.

What to do? As much as he hated the idea, Barlow realized his best strategy right now would be to wait. Uriah Collier would have to leave around half-past-five to make the date at The Dancing Bear at six. That would make one less person for him to deal with. If he was lucky, the man would take his bodyguard or son with him.

The problem with that, it would give Barlow only a few minutes until they came upon his van blocking the lane. He would have to enter the house, deal with whoever might be left, find Pet, and get her out of there. If things really went his way, he would find a weapon, maybe a deer rifle.

Remembering the broken lattice work, he decided to get out of the weather under the porch, curl up against the wall of the house, and catch a nap. He would need to be rested when the time came. Finding his way back down the steps and around to the side of the porch, Barlow pressed through the opening and encountered a musky, animal smell. Rats or raccoons may have denned here at one time. The space was high enough for him to stand. Now out of view of the house, Barlow risked using the built-in light on his phone to scan the area.

Metal picnic chairs hung from hooks embedded into the porch stringers. A length of iron pipe, too long to be useful as a weapon, and assorted building materials, cinder blocks, and bricks.

From the far corner of the porch underside came a low growl and a chuffing. Startled, Barlow swung the beam of his light toward the noise. Two big eyes reflected back at him. Barlow gasped as he realized a black bear had been hibernating beneath the porch.

Before he could react, the animal exploded his way. Instinctively, Barlow swung the tire iron catching the beast on the side of the snout. The animal bellowed, knocking Barlow to the ground as it burst past him. The metal chairs fell from their hooks, clattering to the ground, making enough noise to sound like two cars colliding head on. The bear turned, looked at Barlow, and unleashed a horrific roar before tearing through the flimsy lattice and escaping into the night.

41

CHAPTER 41

Howie Boy Collier snapped awake at the terrible sound. For a moment, he feared the entire lodge would come crashing down around him. "What the hell was that?"

He sprang from his recliner and ran to the rifle cabinet. His father kept the key on top. Howie Boy felt for and found the key, speared it into the lock, and opened the glass door fronting the cabinet. Grabbing his father's twelve gauge shotgun with one hand, he opened the drawer beneath and pulled a box of shells with his other hand. He loaded the shotgun and stuck a few more rounds in his trouser pocket.

Feeling more confident, he took a moment to process what he had just heard. There had been a growling, or was that just his imagination? He had been drinking a lot today and still felt a bit tipsy. Was a bear prowling around outside? He walked into the utility room and opened the breaker panel. He switched on all the exterior lights, knowing it would light up the area around the lodge like a Christmas tree. The illumination would scare off any nearby bear.

For a moment, he had the uneasy feeling that somehow Barlow Jackson might have figured out his location from their brief phone call. He laughed. No way. He chided, "You're spooking yourself, Howie Boy."

Still, he remained uncomfortable. He walked across the living room and opened the front door. "Oh, holy hell, it's snowing." That was an unexpected pain-in-the-ass. If this was the start of a bad cold snap, the ground might freeze making it hard for him to dig the hole he needed to dispose of the bodies. If the storm kept up, it would make digging a sloppy mess in the morning.

He cursed his bad luck. Howie Boy closed the door and grabbed his coat. It would be better if he dug the hole now instead of dealing with who knew how much snow accumulation in the morning. He buttoned up and grabbed his hat.

Better check on the lady cop. It wasn't likely she would try anything, but he wanted to make sure she was still secured in her room.

He closed the gun cabinet, but didn't bother locking it, and climbed the staircase to the second floor. He unlocked her door. She lay on the bed sleeping in the exact same position he had left her, the oxy pills having done their job. He watched her for a few moments thinking again what a waste it was that she would have to die.

He backed out and locked her in.

The backhoe was parked at the back of the lodge under a shed that had been constructed to keep firewood dry. He wanted to get the job done as quickly as possible so he could get back to sleep. Tomorrow would be even more stressful than today.

Barlow lay on his back gasping, waiting for his hammering heart to calm from his bear encounter. He mumbled, "That was way freakier than anything that ever happened to me in the Middle East." He hoped nothing like it would ever happen again. Luckily, the bear was probably more frightened than he was and thought only of making an escape. Good thing it wasn't a mother with cubs.

He sobered after realizing anyone in the house would now be awake. He needed to get out of there. With wobbly legs, he stood and considered his next best move. Someone would likely come to investigate. Where could he hide?

The woods. Barlow left the shelter beneath the porch and felt big, thick flakes of snow pelt his face. An inch already covered the grass. While making his way across the yard, lights snapped on illuminating the entire area like a baseball stadium at night. He sprinted for the trees and ducked behind a thick trunk. After catching his breath, Barlow peeked around the tree. Nobody had come outside yet.

After about five minutes, he wondered if the lights would remain on all night until morning with no way for him to make his way back to the house without being seen. He shivered, unsure if it was from the cold or from the lingering effect of his near-death experience with the bear.

He noticed the man who had been in the recliner stepping onto the porch, bundled up in a camo hunting coat and carrying what appeared to be long-barreled shotgun. The man looked around and stomped off the porch toward the back of the house.

Barlow watched, unable to do anything as long as the guy carried the shotgun. He disappeared behind a shed and rack of firewood. An engine started, some sort of heavy equipment. What was this guy up to?

He came into view driving a backhoe and headed for the far corner of the clearing. There he stopped and started to dig.

"Why is the crazy fool digging at this time of night and during a snowstorm?" Barlow scanned the house. How many more men were inside? Given the distraction caused by the backhoe, he decided to risk crossing the yard under the glare of spotlights to peek into some windows.

When he reached the busted-up lattice work, Barlow caught his breath and worked himself around to the porch. He waited a moment until sure no one else was in sight and climbed the stairs. He tried the knob.

This time it was unlocked. The door opened with a creak. Barlow stepped back. Everything remained quiet, so he ducked inside and closed the door behind him. Taking a moment to scope out the lodge's rustic charm, he spied the gun cabinet. He tiptoed over and slid open the glass doors, pulled out a Winchester lever action .30-30 rifle and smiled.

"This is a game changer," he mumbled.

From the drawer beneath the gun rack he found half a box of shells, ten rounds. He slid five into the rifle's tubular magazine and levered a round into the chamber. The other five rounds he pocketed. No longer needing the tire iron, he slid it under the gun cabinet out of sight.

Still no activity from anywhere within the house. The muffled engine noise from outside assured Barlow that recliner man continued digging with the backhoe.

Recalling his Marine training and taking great care, he cleared every room on the first floor. Where was old man Collier? Where was Pet? He discovered the interior door to the basement and found nobody down there. If anyone else was home, they would be on the second floor.

He climbed the stairs, leading with the business end of the rifle. From the second-floor landing, he could see four doors hanging open and one closed. He tried the closed door. Locked. He wanted to call out Pet's name but couldn't risk it until he cleared the other rooms.

The backhoe engine grew louder, recliner man apparently returning to the house from whatever he had been doing. That left Barlow with a dilemma. He felt certain Pet was behind the locked door, but he needed to clear the rest of the upstairs rooms to make sure no one else could interfere with her rescue.

When the backhoe motor shut off, Barlow knew he was out of time. He moved into the nearest open bedroom and checked the closet. All clear. The creaking front door and footsteps confirmed for Barlow that recliner man had returned.

Footsteps sounded on the staircase.

Recliner man was coming.

42

CHAPTER 42

While digging a grave at the far edge of the clearing, Howie Boy reconsidered his strategy. He originally intended to meet this Barlow Jackson character at six the next morning, kill him, bring him back to the lodge and dump him into the grave. Then he would do the same to the lady cop. She had been insurance in case Barlow didn't show up.

The snowstorm threw a monkey wrench into those plans. If it kept dropping snow at the rate of an inch an hour, he might not be able to make it back up the mountain. Even if he did, he had no desire to be snowed in by himself for who knew how long.

Nope. He would kill the lady cop now and leave; take his chances Barlow would make it to the meeting. If that didn't happen, Howie Boy felt confident he'd find another way. He always did.

No sense shedding his coat and boots since he'd be going right back outside. He left the shotgun on the deck of the backhoe. No way was he going to splatter blood all over the walls of the room. He would shoot her outside. Howie Boy smiled at his ability to think things through. He had it all figured out. He was a planner.

Howie Boy unlocked her bedroom door and entered. He approached the lady cop, grasped her shoulder and shook. "Hey. Wake up."

She made a mewling sound and opened her eyes. Closed them.

He shook her again. "C'mon, we have to go. Get up." Sliding a hand beneath her back, he tried to lift her. She was soaking wet from perspiration. Feeling her forehead, he discovered she was burning up with fever.

"No," she pleaded. "Leave me alone. I hurt."

Howie Boy considered the irony. He was about to kill this woman but also worried about how much pain she was in, feeling sorry for her.

He decided he didn't have time to feel sorry for her. Grabbing both of her wrists, he hoisted her into a sitting position. Two things happened simultaneously. The lady cop vomited causing him to recoil in disgust, and he felt a hard, blunt object poke him in the middle of the back.

Startled, he whirled around and gawked at a man pointing a rifle at his chest. "Who the hell are you?"

"Where's your father? Which room is he in? Who else is here with you?"

Howie Boy quickly figured it out. He had led Barlow Jackson to believe his father had spoken with him on the phone and made the arrangements. Somehow Barlow tracked him down and had gotten the drop on him. Howie Boy also recognized an opportunity to reverse the odds.

"He's at the end of the hall." He raised an arm and pointed in the general direction. Just as he suspected, Barlow shot a glance that way. When he did so, Howie Boy made his move.

He grabbed the rifle barrel with both hands and tried wrenching it from Barlow's grasp. The action caused Barlow to tighten his grip on the trigger and the weapon fired. The deafening crack of a rifle shot detonating in a confined space had a similar effect as a flash-bang grenade, disorienting both men.

The rifle dropped to the floor.

From somewhere behind him, Howie Boy heard the lady cop scream, but he couldn't be sure. Both his ears were ringing. He shook his head to clear his senses and noticed Barlow doing the same. The rifle lay on the floor between them, but it was closer to Barlow. If they both dove for it, Barlow would get there first.

Instead of lunging for the gun, he used a football move and launched himself at Barlow, driving his head into the other man's chest, his forward momentum causing Barlow to fall backward, crash into a chest of drawers, and crumble to the ground.

Howie Boy turned and went for the rifle. While bending to pick it up, he felt Barlow grip both his ankles and yank his feet out from under him. He got his hands in front just in time to prevent landing on his face. Barlow was crawling over his back, pawing for the rifle. Howie Boy shot out an arm and shoved the rifle under the bed. It clattered against the far wall, out of reach.

Barlow rolled off and tried to stand, but Howie Boy was quicker. Realizing that Barlow stood between him and the rifle, he scrambled out of the bedroom, a new strategy in mind. It was going to take Barlow at least a minute to move the bed and get to the rifle, plenty of time for him to run down the stairs and out the back door before Barlow could shoot at him. Plenty of time to retrieve to his shotgun.

How did Barlow manage to track him down? It didn't matter, in fact, it couldn't have turned out better. He had both of them now. Barlow coming here had made his job a whole lot easier. Everything always worked out to his advantage.

Barlow allowed Howie Boy Collier to go. He'd deal with the man later. Right now, he needed to help Pet. She looked awful. Her purple bruises now appeared mottled pale. She was clammy with wide unfocused eyes. She lay back on the bed staring at the ceiling, trembling.

He bent over her and placed his hands on both sides of her face. The heat she gave off scared him. She had to be suffering from a massive injury or infection. "Pet, what happened? What did that bastard do to you?"

He could see her struggle trying to focus on him. She swallowed. Her strained voice sounded barely above a whisper. "Barlow, is that really you?"

"Of course. The Find-my-iPhone app worked. C'mon, I'm going to get you out of here."

She coughed and tears leaked from the corners of her eyes. "Can't. I'm all busted up inside. Too much pain. Barlow, I'm dying. I'm so sorry. This time it's going to be me who leaves you."

"Don't talk like that. Please, Pet, try to stand."

She grimaced in pain. "It feels like my whole torso is on fire. I'm having trouble breathing." She gripped the blanket and writhed. "I can't stand it, Barlow. Help me to die to find relief from this agony. Let me go. Just let me go."

Rising panic welled within him. She was obviously in big trouble, but he would not let her give up. He would never again let her go. Squeezing both of her shoulders, he shouted. "You are NOT going to die on me, Petronia Henning. Fight." He shook her. "Fight, damn it. You have to hold on until I get you to a hospital."

She flashed a rueful smile but said nothing. She closed her eyes.

From the doorway behind him, Barlow heard one of the most intimidating sounds in the world, the snick-snick of a round being chambered into a pump action shotgun.

43

Chapter 43

Barlow turned and found Howie Boy leveling a shotgun at his face. If he pulled the trigger, it would blow his head clean off. He had underestimated the man, figuring he would get in his vehicle and flee. Barlow did the only thing he could do at the moment and raised his arms in surrender.

Howie Boy's expression remained totally neutral, same with the tone of his voice. "Here's what's going to happen. You're going to pick up the lady and carry her downstairs. As long as you're carrying her, you won't be able to do anything stupid."

"Carry her where?"

"I'll tell you. Let's go. Be quick about it."

Barlow turned to Pet, slid one arm under her legs, the other under her shoulders. She shuddered when he lifted her and started sobbing.

Barlow tried soothing her. "Shhh, put an arm around my neck."

She couldn't manage even that much and went quiet. Barlow guessed she had passed out from whatever pain she suffered. Although Pet was slender and had a great physique, she was dead weight. For the first time in his life, Barlow silently thanked his father for making him haul heavy bundles of shingles up ladders. It had developed his upper body strength making it possible for him to move her.

He carried her down the staircase taking care to not trip. Howie Boy followed behind. When they reached the bottom, he motioned with the end of his shotgun toward the door. "Outside."

So far, that was exactly what Barlow would've done in getting help for Pet, but he wasn't naïve enough to think Howie Boy would volunteer to drive them to the hospital. He stepped onto the porch. Three inches of snow had now accumulated on the grass, and it continued to fall relentlessly.

"Across the meadow, toward the far corner," Howie Boy ordered.

Barlow guessed the plan. Howie Boy had dug a hole as a grave. He meant to shoot them and bury their bodies. The knowledge should have filled him with fear. Instead, it gave him purpose. He had to figure a way out during the time it took to walk through the snow to the hole in the ground.

He could think of only one thing to do, and as tactics went, he knew it was pretty lame. But it was his only move. "I need to stop to take a rest. Pet is getting heavy."

"Keep walking," Howie Boy ordered.

"Seriously, man, I'm afraid I'm going to drop her." After saying that, Barlow faked like he was stumbling and went to his knees. Gently as possible, he laid Pet on the ground. He wasn't out of breath but pretended like he was and panted.

Pet moaned and trembled. Her eyes remained closed.

Barlow looked up at Howie Boy, gauging the distance between them. About ten feet. The man still had the shotgun pointed in his general direction, but he seemed more relaxed, as if confident. "Let me take off my coat and put it on her. She won't last long out here in the condition she's in."

"Pick her up," Howie Boy said with more heat in his voice than before. "In a few minutes she's not going to feel anything."

"I don't suppose there's any sense trying to reason with you."

"I said, pick her up."

Barlow sighed, faking resignation. "Okay, okay." He reached for Pet. While sliding his hands toward her, he scooped hands full of the wet, clumpy snow. They made tight, compact snow balls in his fists.

He swiveled his head toward Howie Boy. "Before you kill us, I'm hoping you'll do me the courtesy of answering one question." Barlow had no question. His statement was meant to mentally distract the man.

Before Howie Boy could respond, Barlow threw both snowballs in rapid succession. The first one sailed by his ear; the second caught him square on the forehead stunning him. Knowing he had only a split second, Barlow sprang up like a jack-in-the-box and went straight for the other man's knees. He tackled Howie Boy causing him to topple over backward. He heard him make a sound like, "Oof," and knew he had knocked the wind out of him. The shotgun fell from Howie Boy's grasp. For good measure, Barlow punched him in the jaw and saw the light go out of his eyes.

He gulped air and calmed himself. Letting the shotgun lay, he grabbed Howie Boy by the feet and dragged him toward the hole. The snow acted as lubrication, making the job almost effortless.

As they neared the hole, Howie Boy started coming to. He wheezed. "What are you doing?"

Barlow dropped him at the edge of the hole. "Where are the keys to your vehicle?"

"Why?"

Barlow kicked him in the ribs.

Howie Boy gasped. "In the ignition. Look, my father is a bottomless pit of cash. He'll give you whatever you want."

"Speaking of pits." Barlow rolled him over the side and into the hole.

Howie Boy landed with a satisfying thump and a yelp. "Wait! This hole is over my head deep and not braced. It could collapse. Don't leave me like this. I'll never get out on my own."

Barlow glanced down at the figure at the bottom. "It won't collapse unless you try climbing out. Wait quietly until the cops come for you."

"Goddamn it, I am Howie Boy Collier, the next governor of Idaho. You can't do this to me."

Barlow leaned over the hole. "Yeah? Well, I just did." He turned and ran toward Pet, a lump on the ground now covered by a gossamer veil of snow. He leaned over her and brushed flakes from her face.

She moaned.

"Thank God, you're still with me." He picked her up and quickly moved toward Howie Boy's vehicle.

The man hadn't lied. The keys were in the ignition. Barlow laid her in the backseat, removed his coat and covered her, tried making her as comfortable as possible. He climbed into the driver's seat and turned on the engine. He took off, not bothering to wait for the engine to warm.

"I'll try to be gentle as possible, but I'm going to need to drive fast to get you the help you need. The way out of here is rough." He wasn't sure she could hear him but sensed if Pet didn't have his voice to cling to, she would slip away. He still didn't know what the bastard had done to her.

He sideswiped his van, squeezing past, breaking off both vehicles' side mirrors. It would take an hour to drive to the hospital given the weather. "Hold on, Pet."

When they bounced over an unusually large hole, she groaned. To Barlow's ears, it was sweet music. She was still with him.

He needed to keep talking. "The bus shelter you and I helped your father build, I noticed is in need of repair. There are a lot more homes along our old road, so I imagine kids are still using it. Do you remember us building it? We were what, maybe nine at the time? Yeah, I think it was fourth grade."

Barlow recalled the autumn morning as if it were yesterday. "You were into bandannas at the time. That day you wore a blue paisley one, the back of your hair in pigtails. Your dad was laying shingles over a four by eight plywood sheet serving as our roof. You asked if you could climb up and help him."

Remembering the incident brought a smile to his face. "Your dad joked with you and said he'd let you help if you could prove to him you could drive a nail straight. You bent over, gosh you had skinny little legs back then. You picked a roofing nail from the box and handed it to me."

Even then, Pet had been his best friend, and Barlow knew how special she would always be to him. "You told me to hold the nail for you against the wall so you could show your daddy. The roofing hammer was heavy and you needed two hands to hold it. I was scared you would whack my thumb and told you so."

He flashed back and saw little Pet, hands on her hips, scowling at him. "You promised me you wouldn't miss, remember?"

He giggled. "Stupid me. I held the nail. You reared back and closed your eyes. I think you know what happened next."

Barlow sure did. "I hopped around holding my bashed thumb. I yelled at you for closing your eyes. You accused me of moving the nail and said it was my fault."

A lump formed in his throat at the fond memory and from his desperation to keep her alive. Realizing he needed to fully concentrate on driving the treacherous roads, he refocused. "Stay with me, Pet. I love you so much. Don't leave me."

44

CHAPTER 44

How often, Barlow wondered, had he seen on TV programs a family anxiously waiting in the emergency room for the outcome of a surgery on a loved one? The waiting, the pacing, the jerking of heads toward approaching doctors, frantic to hear any news. On the TV screen, those scenes constituted a classic cliché, yet here he was living the melodrama, feeling the same desperation the actors portrayed.

When he had arrived at the hospital, Pet was barely alive and unresponsive. Her vitals were weak, the ER doctor's face grim. Barlow hadn't been able to tell them much; he knew only that she had experienced excruciating pain in her stomach region.

He had called Mrs. Henning who now waited with him. Barlow told her everything he knew. He had also contacted the state police barracks about Howie Boy. It didn't take long until both Lieutenant Jardine and Trooper Johansson arrived. With Pet's life on the line Barlow figured it didn't matter much anymore whom he could trust.

Barlow gave them a complete accounting from beginning to end. Lieutenant Jardine immediately dispatched a pair of troopers to pick up Howie Boy from the hole in the ground where Barlow had left him. The lieutenant was angry over Pet not letting him know her hobby case was so politically sensitive. He admitted to Barlow how hurt he was that Pet hadn't trusted him.

"It wasn't so much a matter of trust," Barlow told him. "She figured if you knew, you would order her to stand down."

He pointed a finger at Barlow. "Damn right! I absolutely would have."

"And then we would never know. The Colliers would've gotten away with the murder of Neil Mantener."

The point hadn't mollified Pet's boss. "The two of you poking around resulted in the additional murder of a retired detective and the attempted murder of Petronia."

Trooper Johansson admitted to Jardine that Pet had asked him about the meaning of an administratively closed case. He beat himself up over not pressing her on the issue.

It was obvious to Barlow from the demeanor of both men, they cared a lot about her.

Although his mind was on Pet, one thing nagged at him. "What happens now? The Colliers have a lot of clout. Any chance they're going to wriggle out of this?"

Lieutenant Jardine fielded his question. "I'll be charging Howie Boy with kidnapping, assault, and attempted murder of a law enforcement officer. That much will definitely stick. I will also personally notify authorities in the State of Idaho and provide them with all the details. I'll even contact the media in Boise. I'm sure some enterprising journalist will see to it the citizens of that great state will become well-informed about the activities of their gubernatorial candidate. He'll be finished as a politician."

Jardine sighed. "As for the things that happened in the past and the death of Neil Mantener, that will be up to the district attorney. I promise you, I'll do everything possible to have the case reopened, officially this time."

It had been in the early morning hours, maybe around four when Barlow arrived at the hospital with Pet. A quick check of the current time showed half past noon. Pet had been in surgery for a long time.

A short time later, a doctor shuffled into the waiting room, dressed in scrubs, an obvious weariness in his face. The man looked like he needed coffee. Either that or a good stiff drink. "Who is here for Petronia Henning?"

Barlow, Pet's mother, and the two law enforcement officers stood. The doctor motioned for them to remain in their seats. "Petronia is in critical condition, but she's stable."

Mrs. Henning shot a hand to her mouth and started to cry.

"I won't sugarcoat it," the doctor went on. "The next twenty-four hours are going to be touch and go. Her injury was life threatening, but she's a young woman and strong. I'm optimistic."

"What happened?" Barlow asked.

"She suffered a ruptured spleen, likely from a severe blow. The resulting internal bleeding and subsequent infection..." He paused and shook his head. "She was a mess inside. The infection also spread to her pancreas. I can't even imagine the pain she experienced."

Petronia's mother sobbed and blew her nose. Barlow draped his arm around her.

"The damage wasn't repairable. We had to perform a splenectomy," the doctor explained. "A person can live without a spleen, but Petronia is going to have to make some life changes. She will be susceptible to infections for the rest of her life. Her liver will be assuming the duties of her spleen, so she's going to have to take special care to protect that organ. Obviously, she'll have to limit her alcohol intake from now on."

Lieutenant Jardine cleared his throat. "Will she be able to resume her duties as a state police trooper?"

The doctor ran a hand through his hair. "In time. She won't be able to do anything physical for many weeks, if not months."

Between sobs, Mrs. Henning asked, "Can I see my daughter?"

"She's sedated and will be for some time, but yes. You can have a brief visit."

Barlow watched as the doctor led her away.

The two troopers stood. Jardine addressed Barlow. "We're going to be on our way for now, but we'll be back later. I want to be involved with Howie Boy's interrogation."

From the veteran officer's steely expression, Barlow knew the interrogation would be long and unpleasant for Howie Boy. He wished he could be there too. He wanted to beat the man to death with his bare hands over what he had done to Pet.

After the troopers left, Barlow waited for Mrs. Henning. Some time later she finally emerged looking somber. "I barely recognize her. She looks so small and diminished."

Barlow embraced her. "You heard the doctor. She's young and strong. She'll get through this."

Petronia's mother freed herself from his embrace. "Go on. I know you want to see her. I'll wait here for you."

A floor nurse directed Barlow to Pet's room. He entered feeling apprehensive. Mrs. Henning had been spot on. She looked small with all the attached tubes, monitors, and oxygen mask. Barlow bent and kissed her forehead. He pulled up a visitor chair, sat, and took her hand.

"Hello, Pet. I'm sorry for what you are enduring. I'm sorry for asking you to get involved in the first place." He thought about the night of their breakup, long ago. "I'm sorry for everything you suffered because of me."

Barlow realized how tired he was, having been up for over twenty-four very intense hours. He closed his eyes, then opened them, worried he might fall asleep. He sighed. "I never thought

I'd be moving back to Perry County and taking over Dad's company. Ten years ago, I would've told you it would never happen."

Barlow's return and solving of the mystery surrounding that fateful night made him contemplate whether he and Pet were actually destined to be, brought together again by some higher power. "Petronia Henning, I want you in my life. I need you. That is, if you still want me." He paused. "Will you give us a second chance?"

She was sedated and couldn't hear his words, but Barlow could swear she squeezed his hand.

45

CHAPTER 45

Using a box cutter, Pet sliced open a bundle of shingles. She stepped from the back of Barlow's van and wiped her brow. The March afternoon was uncharacteristically warm. Barlow waited patiently for her on top of the roof of the school bus shelter. She lifted three sheets of shingles up to him. That was all she could handle at one time. It amazed her how Barlow could carry an entire bundle under his arm up a ladder and onto a roof. Her man certainly was strong. "Three!"

It had been his idea to rebuild the shelter from the ground up, making it twice the size of the original. "More houses along our old road means more kids," he had said.

The workout from knocking down the old structure and constructing the new one did her good. Having been laid up for weeks and then on doctor ordered limited physical activity caused her muscles to atrophy; she needed to rebuild her strength. This project provided the perfect activity for her to do so. It wasn't lost on her how rebuilding the shelter was also symbolic of the rebuilding of her relationship with Barlow.

During her recuperation, he continuously reassured her how he would never leave her again. Her heart filled with joy over hearing those words, and Barlow had proven his love by having rushed to her rescue, facing death, and driving her to safety during the worst snowstorm of the winter.

Howie Boy remained in prison without bail while awaiting trial. With all the resources at his family's disposal, the DA argued how he would be a flight risk. The judge agreed. Uriah Collier had suffered a stroke and would spend the rest of his days in a wheelchair. He was old, and the stroke may have resulted from natural causes, but Pet wanted to believe the stroke had been caused by seeing his only son and heir fall from grace.

Barlow stopped hammering. "Hey, quit slacking and keep up with me."

She rolled her eyes in mock indignation and handed up another three sheets. "Slave driver."

"It's good practice," he said, "for when we build our own house."

They had pooled their money and bought a corner lot in the New Bloomfield housing development. Barlow's construction crew was due to break ground any time now.

She watched as Barlow nailed the shingles in-place, admiring him.

He stopped and said, "That'll do it. Only thing left is the ridge cap."

Pet raised a hand to her forehead, shielding her eyes from the sun. "Why don't you come down and take a break?"

"Don't mind if I do." He descended the short ladder, and Pet handed him a bottle of water from the cooler.

"Thanks." He twisted the cap and gulped it down. He ran his hand along the smooth exterior of the shelter. "I'm glad we decided to go with vinyl siding instead of the original T-111 material. This shelter should last a good long time."

"I hope the kids appreciate it."

"If they don't, I'm sure their parents will."

The structure looked neat and trim, but Pet had something else on her mind. "Let's sit in the shade."

Barlow followed her inside the shelter. They had built-in benches running the length of the interior walls for the kids to sit while waiting for the school bus. The wall facing the road had a three-foot opening as an entrance and exit.

Pet grabbed Barlow's hand and pulled him down beside her onto one of the benches. She looked into his eyes. "Remember the afternoon we did it in the old shelter?"

"How could I forget."

"Think we should christen this one?"

Barlow chuckled. "In broad daylight? Anyone driving down the road and glancing in would get quite an eyeful."

"You wouldn't have hesitated back then."

"Yeah, when we were kids. We're responsible adults now." He tapped a finger against her healed nose. "Must I remind you Petronia Henning that you are a Pennsylvania State Police Trooper? It wouldn't look good for you to literally be caught with your pants down."

She and Barlow had discussed her career. After everything that happened, Pet had second thoughts about staying in law enforcement. If Barlow had asked her to pursue another line of work, she would've considered it. Instead, he supported her, told her to follow her dream of becoming a detective or a forensic scientist. The man was a prince.

Being a trooper was risky, a roll of the dice every day she reported for duty, especially now that she had to be more vigilant with her health. As Barlow reminded her though, many of her brethren spent their entire tenure in law enforcement without ever having to draw their weapon.

She decided to stick with it for now. Nothing in life was permanent; she could always change her mind later.

Barlow looked pensive. "I think we should leave the honors of christening this place to the new generation of students. Let them make new memories here." He faced her with a twinkle in his eye. "When we get home, though, I'm going to accept your invitation."

By home, he meant her apartment. Barlow had moved in with her shortly after her discharge from the hospital.

"In the meantime." He leaned in and kissed her. "Consider that an appetizer."

The kiss warmed her inside. She smiled, feeling certain there would soon be a ring in her future. A new one. She had finally shed her old wedding band permanently. Last week, she caught Barlow studying the jewelry ads in the Sunday newspaper. Either he didn't know she was watching, or he pretended not to notice.

Barlow got up from his seat. "I think it's time for the finishing touch. I'll be right back."

He left her sitting inside the bus shelter but returned in less than a minute carrying a hammer, box of nails, and a plaque. She had been with Barlow when he ordered the plaque and thought it was a sweet thing for him to do. He held it against the back wall. "Does this look like it's centered?"

She stood and inspected his placement. "Hmm, maybe a little to the right."

Barlow made the adjustment.

"That looks good," she said. The plaque read:

Dedicated to the Memory of Forrest Jackson.

While Barlow held the plaque in-place, he said, "Ironic, isn't it? I couldn't wait to get away from my old man, and now I want to honor him. Anyway, I misjudged my father. He might have been a son-of-a-bitch, but he never killed anyone. He played his part in making me into the man I am today."

Barlow glanced at her. "Hold the plaque while I nail it into place."

Pet grabbed the hammer. "Let me do it. You're already holding it in the perfect spot."

His eyes went wide in alarm. "Are you crazy? After the last time you whacked me in the thumb, no way."

She scoffed. "We were in fourth grade. C'mon, are you ever going to forgive me for what happened way back then?"

"How do I know you're any better at hammering now than you were back then?"

Pet couldn't help but giggle. She pulled a nail from the box. "You'll just have to trust me." She placed the nail against the top center of the plaque. "Hold it here."

"My thumbnail was black for weeks afterwards," he reminded her.

"Don't be such a baby. Hold the nail."

He eyed her suspiciously and held the nail. "Be sure to focus."

"I'm not a little girl anymore. I can handle this."

"Pet, don't you dare miss."

"Oh, shut up."

"I'm just saying."

"Don't move. If you do, it won't be my fault if you get whacked."

"See, you're already making excuses."

"Okay, Barlow, here goes. On the count of three." She gripped the hammer in her hand. "One." She lined up her shot. "Two." She raised the hammer.

CPSIA information can be obtained
at www.ICGtesting.com
Printed in the USA
LVHW040104060123
736479LV00011B/859

9 781944 253486